Josie Barnard has been an editor, journalist and radio broadcaster. Her first novel, *Poker Face*, published by Virago was the winner of a Betty Trask Award.

Praise for *Poker Face*

'Barnard's short sharp sentences are like shards of glass' *Guardian*

'Extremely moving' *Financial Times*

'A nose for hidden sadness' *New Statesman*

'Unsentimental, sometimes disturbing and unforgettable' *The Good Book Guide*

Also by Josie Barnard

Poker Face

the pleasure dome

Josie Barnard

Virago

A *Virago* Book

Published by Virago Press 2002
First published by Virago Press 2000

Copyright © Josie Barnard 2000

The moral right of the author has been asserted

A CIP catalogue record for this book
is available from the British Library.

ISBN 1 86049 761 6

Typeset in Ehrhardt by M Rules
Printed and bound in Great Britain by
Clays Ltd, St Ives plc

Virago Press
An imprint of
Time Warner Books (UK)
Brettenham House
Lancaster Place
London WC2E 7EN

www.virago.co.uk

the

pleasure

dome

for Stephen

Acknowledgements

With thanks to Lennie Goodings,
Cat Ledger and Susan Schulman.

The shadow of the dome of pleasure
Floated midway on the waves;
Where was heard the mingled measure
From the fountain and the caves.
It was a miracle of rare device,
A sunny pleasure-dome with caves of ice!

SAMUEL TAYLOR COLERIDGE, *Kubla Khan*

chapter 1

*L*ast night, in the final pub Belle crawled to, the barman cared because she spilled three pints and he had to clear the mess up afterwards. Then the taxi-driver took such interest that he refused to give her a ride at all. Swaying in her twisted blouse and pencil skirt, Belle remonstrated through the window he was winding up, 'I *never* vomit. My sh-tomach is like *iron*.'

Crawling out of bed now, at 9 am, she braces an arm against the wall and clutches the other to her head. Shards of glass stab out through her eyes.

She pulls on a shirt, inch by inch. The effort pulses through her temples.

In the bathroom, she lowers her face into a basin of cold water and stares until the plug has settled and the numbness feels natural.

She staggers down the hall, but the process of getting into a suit works like scaffolding. She fumbles to do up her shirt buttons, buckles her trousers' belt more assuredly, and by the time she has pulled on her jacket she feels quite sturdy.

She slips her hands down the pin-stripes. She fingers the smooth prong of a cufflink but can't yet bring herself to look around.

Belle did try to make her flat look nice.

The living room in particular resisted her attempts to decorate when she first moved in. Strips of lining paper failed to stick, and instead became curlicued tombstones to her efforts on the floor. The ancient wallpaper's intricate motif faded, continued to change over time, seeming to creep like moss. Furniture that looked cheerful enough elsewhere died in here. The sofa became a burial mound, her sewing box a relic.

Dust flies as she pulls a drawer and grabs the scissors. Her fringe has been getting in her eyes. She cuts, chewing with the blades till all the bits that were in her view have drifted to the floor past the cracked hand-mirror she's holding up. She squints at herself in it.

'There. That's better.'

Her hair is jagged up her forehead, splays long at her shoulders – and the carelessness of it only makes her face appear more open.

Her eyes are an especially clear blue within black lashes. The red of her mouth deepens according to her emotions. She applies thick layers of lipstick and mascara. From her box of watches she chooses the plastic one she got free with a pack of cereal.

'And I don't even feel sick any more.'

She slams her front door behind her.

The Underground trip doesn't take long. It is a direct route. At each stop, the whine of protest gets louder until the train is hurtling down the tunnel again.

Between carriage exits, commuters jostle for seats. Belle keeps separate. Even compared to the back-packing tourists she thinks she looks relaxed, dangling in her man's pin-striped suit from an overhead handle, allowing her body to be taken by the rhythm of the journey.

Through childhood, there was one event she always won at her school's Sports Day. She'd do daft balancing acts, crazy leg movements, twist her head the wrong way and turn out to be gold-medal standard. Today's audition could be her adult equivalent.

'My backwards egg and spoon race.'

She smiles.

People tell her she's lucky to be tall. She is not hugely busty, but she's not flat-chested either. Yet the overall impression she gives is oafish. Her own shadow scares her sometimes.

On the street, Belle pushes through the crowds. She loosens her tie. She is in the heart of Soho and it seems to her that every other shop is a porn shop.

Confronted with a photograph of a woman squeezing her tits, spreading her legs, Belle finds that the photography has the effect that was intended. Even those women in the fashion pages of glossy monthlies don't make her want to *be like* them. They make her *want* them.

But then, that's why she's here, isn't it, she thinks as she passes an 'XXX' cinema, her stiff nipples safe behind the thick lapels of her suit.

Xanadu's is perfect: a place where perhaps she will be able to shed her mannishness and come not merely to look feminine but to feel it too.

Xanadu's is in the busiest part of Soho, street market in front, retail outlets and offices teetering on either side. Yet it stands alone, defying a sense of proportion. It is square, not more than four storeys, but it appears to tower, windowless walls rising to catch the sun and become lustrous, the building's flat top seeming to be holding up the sky to let it float, azure chiffon over London.

Belle leaps over a pile of crates and, as instructed, turns down a side alley, which is empty except for the smell of urine. She masks her face with her sleeve and wades deeper.

Sounds from adjacent streets twist over, ropes of communication. Belle is running, yet everything seems still. Her damp hair sticks flat to the back of her neck.

She turns a corner and to her left is a metal door with as many dents as rivets in. At the end of the alley, she sees light. Belle presses the buzzer and the door opens. The lift is as immediate as a cake without icing. Belle steps straight in. The surge of the lift catches her stomach.

When Belle used to win the school's joke race, afterwards she'd get to stand on a podium. There was sniggering, and there was applause.

The doors open and Belle feels she's in a high-rise paradise.

Xanadu's administrative reception area has walls the colour of sandy beaches, adorned with pictures of bikini-clad women. The receptionist sits at a bamboo-edged desk. Belle is standing under the leaves of a potted palm – beside a brown-eyed blonde.

'Are you auditioning too?'

Belle tries to back away.

'I'm Sylvie Gift,' the blonde pursues, flushed, grinning. 'I've been working up to this for months.'

There weren't many challengers at all for the backwards egg and spoon race, let alone seriously enthusiastic ones.

Sylvie grasps the hand Belle has put between them. 'What's your name, then?'

'Belle. But I must be in the wrong place.'

Air-conditioning rattles through the vents.

The receptionist calls, 'Miss George.'

Belle's breath comes out as frost clouds. 'Ms.'

'*Ms* George,' says the receptionist, arching a well-plucked eyebrow. 'Mr Vincent is ready for you.'

Even the light falling through the latticed Perspex ceiling is cold. Sylvie whispers, 'Good luck!'

Ricky Vincent's face is sullen. Standing at the window in his office, he has prised the slats of his blind apart to form a peephole out. A nylon-curtained window in the building opposite advertises 'MODELS'. Below, by a lamp-post a clipper cons some geezer into paying now for sexual services he won't catch her for later. Flashing 'XXX' signs lure punters in to see 'GIRLS GIRLS GIRLS' who'll wiggle their bums for two minutes. It's hype, but effective.

Inside, Ricky Vincent sighs as he sits at his desk. Ticket sales are down this week at Xanadu's.

Auditions used to be a high point for him. His advertisements once read: 'THOSE WITHOUT REFEREES/ REVUE EXPERIENCE NEED NOT APPLY'. His girls can call themselves *artistes*. Pole dancers get huge tips.

Cellulite, short necks and droopy busts are obvious no-no's, but after that, nowadays, he can't be as choosy.

All the same, Ricky Vincent activates his executive desk toy, setting the chrome balls clickety-clack displacing each other. From a drawer he takes a worn tobacco pouch. Chair-back to the door, he yells, 'Come!'

On the way into his office, Belle has a fight with the door. It sticks. She pushes. It lurches from her hands and bangs the wall.

'Sorry,' she murmurs as she presses it closed.

The swivel chair doesn't move. Its back to her is a silhouette.

'I have classical ballet training.'

A set of neat, white fingers stretch out along the chair's chrome arm. 'And your name is?'

'Belle. Belle George.'

The light falling through the blinds slices the floor in front of her. The black leather chair turns. Belle blinks.

She had expected someone older for a start. He must only be in his mid-30s. Ricky Vincent's chin is dimpled. His cheeks are rosy.

'"Belle George",' he says flatly. '"Classical ballet training",' as if he knows it was only two terms aged eight.

His eyes follow a line of perspiration from her hairline to her neck into her collar. He does up the top button of his flowered shirt. His mouth is so full that even with the corners down-turned a smile is lurking as he opens his packet of rolling tobacco.

'Really, I'm supple,' she says.

He flattens a paper with his thumbnail, long, even strokes. His lowered lids are pale unseeing eyes.

Belle pushes her chest out beneath her poplin shirt. 'I have stamina.'

Teasing interconnected strands of tobacco, he addresses his fingernails. 'I always say that this is a West-End show, only a bit more specialised.'

Looking up, he tilts towards her. 'Did you respond to my theatre press advertisement?'

She twists her hair. 'I contacted you on spec.'

He sighs. 'I like girls who show initiative too.'

His fingers slide round and around the half-made cigarette, refining its shape. 'I give a four-week trial period. Once you're trained up, it's two shows a night, six nights a week,' he says, flicking the head off a lighter and sucking the flame through the cigarette. 'It's hard work.'

She is hypnotised by his eyes' dark circles of experience.

'Bloody hard work.' He blows smoke out, fast. 'Are you ready?'

Belle is confused.

'This way!' Ricky Vincent calls out and disappears down yet another corridor lined with name-plated doors and hospitality seats. The route twists and turns deeper into the building. Belle is feeling sick again.

'This way!' he calls.

She could be in any one of the accountancy, publishing, law firms she's ever temped at. She clutches her stomach.

'This way!'

Except Ricky Vincent's voice lures her, seems to suggest that the task of following it can become an end in itself for her. And as she goes, the furniture is changing. The corporate scenery – computer, stack of box-files – seems to be collapsing – lolling angle-poise, side-turned swivel chair – and turning into something more exciting. Abandoned theatre sets are pushed against the walls. They are escapist spacey constructs – a radar screen, a rocket-ship's nose – with bits of old costumes thrown on – satin and tulle.

Belle knocks a tiara down an alien's warhead. Ricky Vincent has slowed to match her pace. His voice is patient.

'This way.'

The lighting dims. Sections of ceiling bud into plaster-cast flowers.

'Come.'

She steps over a silken rope and pushes through a quilted door to find herself in brightness.

In this empty theatre auditorium, on stage, the ceiling is low, cosy, and it sparkles with a silver festoon. Banks of lights point towards her, protecting. Behind her, the sets include an out-sized spear and a safe with gold bars arranged on top.

Belle leans stage left and looks beyond the rose-tinted chandelier to the back of the auditorium at the sound-system. She hasn't felt this secure for years, maybe never before. She twirls a little. The festoon's strings will hold her up. The big black speakers will tell her what to do. She waves cheerfully.

Ricky Vincent is in the lighting box, at the control panel. The equipment is dated. The unwieldy hammerited metal decks give more weight to his actions. With two definitive clicks, the house lights are down and the mini-spots are on, projecting bars vertically. Belle George is in the light cage and, at the top of the hill of seats, Ricky is in darkness.

He props his legs on a seat in front and crosses his arms behind his head as a cushion. Far below, Belle squints.

He can see her. She can't see him.

'Strip,' Ricky commands.

The way his voice echoes it seems the whole blackness is speaking. On the stage, she's in a white void. She swipes for the edge.

'Everything?'

'Naturally,' the blackness calls.

Just as a swim in the outdoor pool in January had seemed like a good idea right up until she was at the pool-side, now, here, the moment has come to take the plunge and her hands are frozen at her side.

High in his velveteen seat, Ricky Vincent taps his forefingers.

Her hangover is getting ready to surge up and explode her head.

'I haven't got all day, you know.'

She tugs. Threads snap. A jacket button bounces down and rolls across the stage. Its tinkling carries on and on, beyond the spotlights, into the same darkness that contains Ricky Vincent.

In her void, Belle suddenly just wants to get this done with, to know for once for sure either way.

The boards' markings include a blue 'V' – 'V' for victory, 'V' for a fingers' 'fuck you' sign. She stands on it, pulls the shirt over her head, kicks her shoes away and shoves her trousers down with her feet while her hands are arm-locked behind her in a struggle to undo her bra-strap and she's muttering, 'Shit – fuck – damn,' till finally the bra twangs free and she's tensing up her muscles, fists gripped, pumping her underarm tendons, to no avail.

Her naked breasts sink down and out. Between them, her stomach bulges over pigeon toes.

In the darkness of the auditorium, Ricky Vincent leans forward.

'Everything,' he reminds her.

Her hands slip under her pants' elastic. Leg holes hit the boards. The auditorium is silent.

Ricky Vincent taps his fingers.

As he grapples along the seats, he calls, 'Turn!'

She shows him her square arse and protruding shoulder blades. Between the spear and safe props, she can see the back wall clearly. She waits.

She begins to feel that her labia, already quite long and purplish between her legs, are growing to dangle even further with the beard of pubes. She clamps her thighs tighter but is now only more convinced her exterior is not the worst of it and eyes from all over the auditorium are probing inside her, sharp as scalpels, to her guts.

Then suddenly, the auditorium is fully lit. She twists.

Ricky Vincent's gone, the door creaking shut behind him. The rows of empty seats are snickering clowns' eyes.

Belle covers both breasts with an arm and grabs for her shirt. She yanks the tongue of her trouser belt. She buries her jacket in her stomach and runs, hunched, an animal in a tunnel that had appeared to be guiding her upwards but plunged. Tears sting as she hurtles down the stairs, into the foyer.

But then, he's here, by a pillar, lighting up a cigarette.

'We can use you.'

'Pardon?'

'You're hired. Come and see the show tonight. First rehearsal tomorrow. I'll be waiting.'

'Here, in this building, for me?'

Outside, Belle does a pirouette – and nearly crashes into a market stall. Brogues skidded off in opposite directions, she pulls upright into one paving stone and coughs. She tucks her hair behind her ears. No one minds. No one even noticed. She's as inconsequential as if she was on one of her night-time benders.

'LAH-VELLY LEMONS,' cries a trader. His barrow, spread with plastic grass, is piled high with waxy-skinned sunbeams. 'TEN FER A POUND. LAH-VELLY LEMONS.'

Belle stares in wonder at the pillar-height light-boxes that flank Xanadu's front entrance. There they are, bare tits and asses on show for all the world to see. Now she is one of the people she referred to as 'they' and – she frowns – the moment of stepping over the boundary was so easy it was almost disappointing. But still – Belle grins – she stepped.

In the middle of Soho, crowds of tourists, workers, families all around her, in an island created by a lime green waste-bin, Belle chooses a vegetable stall as her spot to focus on, pushes up onto her toes and, jaw set, throws herself into another pirouette – and whacks a lamp-post. Hopping about, she shakes her hand, staring at it aghast then clasping it between her knees, biting her lip.

'Damn!'

Now she's given herself a bruise when her body should look tip-top and it's already scarred enough as it is from domestic mishaps – can-openers going out of control, glasses cracking apart as she polished. Though most often what seemed to hit her was the ground.

It would come at her suddenly from an angle. She would be on her trike or bike, pedalling excitedly, her feet still pushing her away when the handles would begin to tip the horizon out of reach, sending her wrist skidding across the cobbles as a brake, furrowing dirt deep into her skin. There was rarely a passerby she could jump to her feet and dust herself down for. So she would lie as she had fallen in the empty stretch of road outside her home, intent on a ladybird's climb to the top of a small weed, or a line of ants in the cracks bearing food and building materials to their queen. When she did get up, she'd pull the bike by its seat, banging and crashing the wheels and handlebars across the cobbles. Later, she might swab the worst cuts and grazes with a piece of soapy toilet paper, or she would simply go to her room and change into a long-sleeved shirt. Then perhaps she'd do a little mending in the living area – secure a shelf, screw a hat peg on more tightly – or go to the kitchen to prepare a midnight snack to leave out – sliced cucumber eyes, carrot nose, tomato mouth smiling in the middle of the plate – or she might stay up herself, crouched behind the sofa, listening for the footfall to check the mood before springing her sock puppets over the top, finger-filled heels and toes jawing praise or solace as necessary.

Belle gained friends and lost them with equal ease. She tried not to show it but she found their concerns petty. Snogging boys wasn't a big deal, she just stuck out her tongue and wiggled, no need to discuss it endlessly at pyjama parties and community hall discos. Instead whenever possible she would follow Lilian in to work – watching, adoring, drifting off afterwards to a lullaby of sophisticated conversation in a Green Room in a pile of strangers' coats, her dreams shaped by the thunder of applause that belonged to someone else.

In a phone booth, Belle finds herself dialling her mother's number.

'Lilian White speaking.'

Belle stands to attention. 'I know you're busy and it's especially stressed at work at the moment, but . . .'

'Do you want a ticket for my show this evening?'

'Actually, I was wondering if I could pop round for coffee.'

'Now? What do *you* think? (Ailsa, for Christ's sake give me another minute!)'

Transmission's always crackly on Lilian's mobile, yet it's possible to hear quite clearly the sounds of people calling for her in the background. Filming is due to start shortly. It is the first of her new television series. She is a chat-show hostess – highbrow.

'I just wanted to tell you, only briefly.' Belle fingers Ricky Vincent's card in her pocket. 'I got the job.'

'At Edenfine and Co? Sweetie, I *am* pleased.'

Belle thumps her forehead. She'd forgotten that was the last one she'd told her mother about. 'In fact . . .'

'Edenfine has a marvellous reputation. Solid, reliable. I know you've had a run of bad luck, but I'm sure this post will last. You'll do fabulously. (Ailsa, two seconds.) Anything else?'

'No.'

'I'm *longing* to hear all your news. Darling, let's speak soon. I'm sorry to be so pressed for time.'

'Good luck for tonight.'

The stress worked up doing the audition has combined with the closeness of the phone booth to slip the watchstrap down Belle's arm to reveal her extra cuff-line, the specks of grit from her childhood falls she didn't get round to washing away suspended in scar tissue, dotting and dashing around her wrist like Morse code. She pushes the watchstrap back to cover them.

Lilian shuts off her mobile.

Ailsa, the PA, is about the same age as her daughter. She is waiting, anxious, awed. Lilian is a role model.

Lilian got in when television was still a new medium. Some producers literally picked good-looking 'chicks' off the street. She is quite low in the media celebrity hierarchy but, even so, she sees the hoops young researchers and assistants have to go through and knows she would never make it now. She wasn't committed. But if it was largely luck, she has no special talents.

'Tell the director,' snaps Lilian, 'I'll be ready in half an hour.'

———

With a paddock on one side, an orchard on the other and a brook at the bottom of the garden, the Knoll was a picture-book version of a happy family home. It was Lilian's through her childhood and a place where Belle spent much of hers. In the holidays she would crouch watching Granny George in the rosebeds doctoring with the secateurs, and then be allowed to have a go herself. Her grandfather enjoyed a bit of recreational design-engineering. The garage became a go-kart workshop, the treehouse an elaborate system of pulleys and platforms for bird-watching and impromptu feasts. Sometimes in the branches they'd star-gaze for what seemed like hours, Belle wrapped with her grandfather in his jacket, embraced in tweed and the scent of his pipe tobacco, his big hands warming hers, elevated in the night sky.

Granny George died. The Knoll was sold. The institution Grandfather George is in now is a low, grey building. It was chosen for its proximity to his daughter. Lilian is only able to cram in the odd visit. Belle calls by every few weeks.

It can still give her the same feelings as the Knoll. Her grandfather is the constant. In the Day Room entrance, her smile is so broad it plumps her cheeks till they are balloons causing her body to float within her pin-stripes.

Her grandfather always looks so stalwart, so *there* in the corner in his armchair, peaked cap pulled to meet the spectacles jutting over his great splodge of a nose.

Just to step across the carpet frees years of composted vegetable odour. Green flock wallpaper harasses red curtains. Bad paintings of mountains clash over spaceship lamps. The decor is so elaborately loud it seems part of a plan to distract from the inmates, who are pushed back in chairs round the edges as if this is a waiting room.

Silence. Lolling heads. No point speaking, or even thinking.

Except for her grandfather, who keeps his walking stick propped ready by his armchair. Belle holds up a potted miniature rose, a bit of living barrier to give him.

'Grandfather!' she calls.

'Lilian!'

This has been going on for months now. Her reflection distorts in her watch face.

'It's me, Belle,' she murmurs hopefully, holding out the pot plant.

He strains to see round the blooms. 'Lilian,' he concludes happily.

Of course she would rather be taken for somebody than nobody. He adores Lilian.

A thread of Belle's suit catches on a thorn. She wraps it round her finger and snaps it off.

The staff will allow him his All-Bran. They confiscate his whisky. The one piece of his own furniture he could fit in his room – a rosewood escritoire in memorial to Granny George – is shoved against the radiator, warping. He was once the smartest of the smart. Now his layers hang emptily, trousers hoiked by braces under his armpits, tweed jacket draping below his knees. It is too hot to have all this on. His body has deferred to his emotional needs, keeping himself in a state of sweaty denial.

He looked after her when Lilian asked him to. Now it's Belle's turn to care for him as much as he'll let her. Bowed on his footstool, her body curved like a receptor, she moves the petals so they hide her face.

'Lilian, Lilian,' he tuts indulgently, shaking his head. 'If I'd said the sky was blue you'd have said it was black.' His lips puff importantly on the pipe he's not allowed any more. 'Science. Academia. I had such plans for you. You'd have made your mark. But you had to do it your own way. Television. So vulgar. Granny George warned me I was being too heavy-handed.'

Belle hears things he'd never have told her when he thought she was herself. She slips her hands up towards her ears but can't quite bring herself to cover them.

'You showed us both. Although, once you'd made your point, you could have stopped.' He frowns. 'You were unconventional enough. I know, you told me – single, independent; relying only on yourself whatever the circumstances. But marriage isn't bad, by no means. Tying the knot might even have made you happy.'

Belle grasps his hands. They're arthritic. His eyes seem to come more into focus.

'She didn't need anybody else. We had each other.' But then, she'd thought she had a part of her grandfather. A vein beneath Belle's iris throbs. 'I'm not your *daughter*, I'm

your *granddaughter*. I was collicky. I screamed. I did projec-
tile vomiting. Lilian couldn't cope at first. But Granny
George could.'

He extracts his hands.

She murmurs, 'You can't have forgotten those summers
when we'd go for long hikes, just you and me, and we'd
have a pub lunch, and I'd drink a half of shandy, and we'd
consult the reference books and discuss the flora and
fauna . . .'

He drifts into a picture of an Alp, which perhaps he
climbed for real when he was a young man. No chance of
going there now. Crevices and overhangs collude to form a
mocking face. 'Lilian,' he says sadly.

Belle's gifts clutter his side-table; it's *her* postcard sticking out of his breast pocket. 'Grandfather,' she pleads. 'This
plant is for you, from me, Belle. Belle George.'

He doesn't accept gifts from strangers. His hands in his
lap are folded at extreme angles, as if they have already
waved their final goodbye. She feels he's taken a chunk of
herself with him.

Behind his glasses, the rheuminess looks penetrable. She
pulls his hat down to cover the gap. The nurses always say
her visits make a difference. His sock is twisted. She rights
it before leaving.

Half an hour later, Belle is still sitting outside on the wall at
the end of the drive. The miniature rose is tumbled in her
lap. Soil has spilled over her pin-stripes. The stems are bare
of petals, which she is holding in cupped hands.

Nearby, above the green cover of a parked motorbike,

two champagne yellow butterflies are trying to mate. One slotted behind the other, they rise and fall in a flurry of wings.

Belle throws the petal confetti up into the air. It falls beautifully, but the butterflies emerge split by the descending cloud.

————

For several summers from the age of fourteen, Belle worked as a volunteer for CKV – City Kids' Vacation. It seemed to her a straightforward way of helping in theory. The children had deprived inner-city term times. The charity gave them cheap or free fun camping holidays in countryside on the South Wales coast. Belle was rewarded with exhilaration at simply seeing the children out there with little to do but play. Football games were heated. Clouds of butterflies during nature walks could cause fear and wonder.

By an administrative accident, Belle arrived the first time to the job of camp cook, responsible for feeding twenty children plus the other volunteers for a week equipped with only a few ring stoves the strength of Bunsen burners. The snapshot the group leader sent her afterwards – treasured, lost – was of Belle in front of the raised flaps of the main tent in the arms of the children who helped her regularly, all laughing, holding out the gallon pan with the retrospective explanation of why the custard hadn't thickened: a full three inches of burn. Those were the children who took to her most fiercely, and she to them. They were mainly younger, between seven and ten. The stories of what had been left behind came mainly from the older ones. Told in flat tones, they tended to be of physical acts of violence – parents going for each other with kitchen knives – outbursts that the bigger children could respond to, by getting the knife away, by shutting the aggressor out until they were sober. It was the eyes of the younger children and what they couldn't tell that began to prey. If nothing was said, nothing could be done, in which case the holiday could be only superficial. Belle was keen to make a real difference.

The minibus had backed into the field. Doors open, it was being loaded for the fishing trip. The rule was that if a child hadn't done their rota duty – helped wash up, aired the dormitory tents – they couldn't go. The boy who was being forbidden Belle considered one of hers. He was making it worse for himself, shouting, lashing out. At this rate he was going to be grounded for the whole day, and the next too. Her voice soft and low, Belle spoke of the things they could do together on site instead. She concluded that although there wouldn't be another fishing expedition, tomorrow's trip would be equally exciting.

She felt elated. It seemed their bond was so real he accepted from her what he wouldn't take from the others.

She was lifting children up the steps into the minibus. Everyone around her turned to stone. She was still smiling as she followed their eyes, head tipping backwards. The sun had been cut in two and was drifting apart over blackness.

The boy had brought a baseball bat down with all his force. It was a few inches from her skull, caught in the hand of the group leader.

*

Now, at a crossroads, Belle pushes a woman in a wheelchair onto the kerb, noting, 'The weather's nice and hot, isn't it?'

'It makes my neck play up.'

Belle re-crosses the road carrying brown paper packages for a heavily pregnant woman who pats her huge, drum belly and says, 'Everything's an effort. It's like having a central heating system inside you can't switch off.'

A man on a bench has his legs braced as if he is trying to get up.

'Can I help?' Belle asks.

'Help yourself,' says the man and sinks back down.

Except for the fact that the suit is tied with string and he's holding not a walking stick but a child's bike wheel sticking out of a laundry bag, he looks quite like Belle's grandfather, without the smile.

She asks, 'Do you mind if I join you?'

His red-rimmed eyes stay fixed on the pavement.

She finds that her thoughts come tumbling: I mean, he was impressed enough to hire me, which is what I went for, so why do I feel hollow? – a hand gesturing to correct herself – no, not hollow, more *curdling*. I mean, he looked decent enough, but then, I don't know what I was expecting, warts or gnarled joints or something. 'You could even call him handsome' – oops, out loud; her eyes flick sideways.

Beside her, the stranger stays staring at the ground. She clears her throat.

'You listening?'

No response.

She plants her chin in her hands and allows herself to

speak the thoughts – "'We can use you'" – although so inaudibly at first she can hardly hear herself.

'*Use*, that's what he said. But then, that's the way with jobs, isn't it? The employer uses, the employee gets paid, fair exchange – unless you hate the job, I suppose, like at Godwin Inc, which could have led somewhere, maybe, in about three decades, if I'd stayed clinging to that bottom rung licking the shoes above me. It had the right trappings – Georgian-fronted offices; my mother was proud to ring me there – but for all that I could put on the right kind of court shoes, the tights always laddered and the shoes gave me blisters. I felt a fraud. And today was different – sure, I felt curdling, hollow or whatever, but not a plain liar. It was hardly a lengthy interview process. It was more honest: strip; yup, that body will do the job.'

Blushing, her stare is straight on the stranger next to her. He hasn't moved. She blows her cheeks out, lowers her voice and eyes again.

'Only, my decisions when I thought they were the *right type* just didn't seem to get me anywhere – except into worse flats in worse areas. And being sacked, or "let go", not just once either, when I'd tried my best, never knowing for sure if at all what it was I'd done wrong, well, it got to me. And this can't be more wrong than anything else in terms of my CV because I haven't a clue where I want my CV to lead. I guess,' she addresses the stranger's knees quizzically, 'I just want to ask someone who's objective if I'm doing the right thing. But then . . .' she trails off. 'Why should you care?'

His head leers her way. She blanches. His gaze slips back towards the ground.

Belle's not as close now, but she's still only an arm's length away.

There is a piece of loose skin at the edge of one of her fingernails. It is small, insignificant, yet when she pulls – carefully, painfully – more keeps coming and she keeps on pulling until she has extracted a section of cuticle root. The skin itself is white. The place it came out is livid but not bleeding. Tomorrow it will be sore, pus swelling in the hole Belle has created.

She checks her watch and leaps up.

'Christ!'

———

The road to Xanadu's is narrow. Its buildings are between only two and five storeys high yet there is no evidence of anything behind, no pointy roofs, no chimneys. Planed off flat, it seems the façades are all there is. And it's not a thoroughfare. Retailers pull wooden barrows about within the street's parameters. Pedestrians move between shops, cafés, back and forth. Heat forces wide-legged, wide-armed ambles. There is a whiff of fairgrounds, bulbs strung under market stalls' canopies giving the fruit and veg displays no shadows – oranges appear to be stacked vertically on top of apples on top of lemons. First-floor mirrored windows reflect mirrored windows. Pigeons perch on invisible ledges.

The sky is fading and stalls are being packed away. Staff coming out of offices loosen ties and walk quickly away from the cloying rotten scent rising from discarded fruit that has rolled into the gutters. All the signs are that the day has ended.

But even behind a pillar, Belle isn't out of sight. The remaining light is a permeating lilac, crawling over Tarmac, up into unmarked doorways. Belle's pin-stripes merge, her pale blue eyes become dark.

She flaps her skirt, but doesn't feel cooler. Blinking only leaves her vision gauzy because the heat is her real clothing, head to toe, tailored seamlessly into every cavity. Any movement only tightens its grip.

A bespectacled woman tells her colleagues, 'I'm staying late tonight,' as she re-enters a dully corporate-looking door. Belle smiles. Xanadu's entrance is framed with fairy lights.

Then suddenly she is sent flying into the street, stumbling over the ground. The fire exit she was leaning against, Peepland's, has been forced open and a jacket sails out followed by a large bare-foot woman in a small top and leggings staggering backwards yelling, '. . . wank myself with a beer bottle? Not if you promise match-money for the tips. Excuse me, but who the hell do you think you are? *Fired?* I QUIT!'

Belle grips the metal of a lamp-post, staring.

'Piss off,' says the proprietor of Peepland. A clutch-purse and pair of ankle boots twist through the air. The door shuts. Hopping to put on one shoe, the woman teeters in a circle of pavement, passers-by repelled equidistantly all around. They give her more than a wide berth. She has her own arena. It could have been a very public humiliation. Belle is ready to cheer. The woman glowers.

'Ignorant shit-heads.'

The audience shuffles back, still transfixed. The woman puts on her other shoe and rises to her full height plus four inches. She pronounces, 'I'm someone's daughter too.'

The crowd breaks up, disturbed and angry. Smiling, the woman tosses her clutch-purse. Its Day-Glo trim catches the street-light, a celebratory Catherine wheel flying through the dark.

Belle thought she knew this area. Another Soho is all around her, ready to be absorbed, wonderland.

'Hello again!'

She turns, heart pounding.

'It's *you*,' the brown-eyed blonde, 'Sylvie . . .'

'. . . at your service.'

'You got the job?'

'And you?'

'We've done it.'

Moving close, Sylvie taps Belle's arm with her copy of *The Stage*. 'I can't believe my luck.' She breathes London in, rosebud mouth gawping. 'I only came down yesterday and I got the first audition I went for.'

Sylvie's face is so fresh from the mould, no lines have been worn in yet. Belle wonders, 'How old are you?'

'Eighteen,' Sylvie replies, averting her gaze. 'Why?'

Even if it's not by much, Belle thinks how nice it is to be older and wiser.

From Xanadu's entrance, behind the glass, a half-naked woman in a leather-studded cap winks at them from a light-box. Lives can change fast round here.

*

At 7.45 pm the glass front doors miraculously open. Individuals dart in, male, most like the cliché with collars turned high, hats tugged low. Nearby, a coach pulls up. Tourists climb out, dozens of them, wives included. Exuberance funnels Belle and Sylvie in.

At the front of the queue, a middle-aged couple look disapproving as two members of staff share a quick joke in an ante-room before taking their posts. Wearing smart tuxedos, the cashiers are cheerily young and male. The desk has one single, black castellation. They sit behind it and the queue becomes a pressing mob. No one faffs about writing cheques or searching in wallets for credit cards. People shove notes at them, fivers and tenners, crumpled. The first customer is addressed warmly.

'Hello again, sir!'

'First time. What's your prices?'

The cashier twists his dicky bow. 'For twenty-five pounds you can sit close to the stage.'

'Ten pounds please.'

Xanadu's street displays are coy compared to the blown-up video stills that fill the windows of surrounding porn shops. Here, in the foyer – with its maroon walls and grandly glittering chandelier – the pictures are more explicit. In the largest lightbox, a body is positioned as if she is a vagina swallowing a shaft of cannon. Her face on top looks pleasantly surprised.

Sylvie's gaze is in Belle's and vice versa. They shuffle forwards with the queue. Sylvie's smile is perky.

'I'm here to get my Equity card.'

Belle nods gladly. The cashier leans round the desk's

castellation, level with them. They're the only single women.

'Comps?' he whispers and has merely to click his fingers and the General Manager, also in a dicky bow and DJ, is whisking them past the queue like princesses, up the chrome-edge staircase.

Crisp black and white in his usher's outfit, the GM gently urges Belle and Sylvie, 'Do enjoy the show.'

In most obvious respects, Xanadu's auditorium is the same as any West End theatre's. It has a stage and an aisle gradually ascending between lines of flip-based seats. It is the details that make the difference. The stage projects far enough to be embraced by the curving first few rows, which have screwed onto their backs not miniature binoculars with which to see more clearly but drinks holders, to allow alcohol to relax the punters' senses. Overhead, house lights are recessed in a ceiling that is close and painted black, creating tunnel vision. The air-conditioning is blasting cold. Belle and Sylvie are distorted, tightly shivering, their faces turned explosive pinks.

A few rows down, three young men in bright Hawaiian shirts glance up at them complicitously. In crossing her legs, Belle knocks Sylvie, who she will soon see naked – and Belle's at the opposite side of her seat, grin twitching upside down, eyes rolling, fingers twisting her hair on end as the house lights dim.

The dark forms a cowl round Belle's face and drapes around her body, over her hands in her lap. The blackness is complete. She can't see anything, not a glint of her watch face, nothing. Having spent so much of her time trying to put her finger on life's fast-forward button, she feels the possibility here that the atmosphere alone could absorb her forever. The rising curtain sparkles with a golden constellation. The music drifts between traditional striptease – lots of jolly piano and plinky-plonky drum rolls – and up-to-the-minute electro beat, the wild mix telling her that she's in a different world.

An extremely proper, mildly amused male voice fills the auditorium, confirming unreality.

'THEY'RE GLAMOROUS, THEY'RE SEXY, *EXTRA*-ORDINARY. ARE YOU READY, LADIES AND GENTLEMEN? FOR YOUR EYES ONLY . . .' – the intonation is game-show hearty – '*ZONE FANTAS-TICA*.'

A dozen girls file on to the apron of the stage, twirl silver-topped canes, take their top hats off, twirl them, and put them back on. They do a bit of clumsy criss-crossing between each other. They're mauvely indistinguishable. They wiggle their notional coat-tails and file off.

Leaning forward in her seat, Belle frowns as if she must have missed something. Just when she'd slowed down, the show is speeding up.

A prop is there from nowhere: a furnace with tonguing paper flames. A girl leaps out in a cap-and-braces saucy stoker outfit, strobing red and orange. The music sharp-cuts and she is stripping, jacket first.

She pulls it back and forth between her legs. She tosses it away. She does some breast manipulation with the braces. She tosses them away.

The music is the stuff migraines are made of. Belle presses fingers to her temples.

And something else is bothering her.

On the apron's edge, two girls play decoy, then they're gone, and so's the furnace. In its place is a tilted section of a baize-type desk, featuring draped on top, of course, a girl.

There hasn't been any applause at all. It was the clapping of innumerable hands that was to make everything worthwhile for her – rapturous, thundering approval.

Belle slides down in her seat until her knees are nudged up into her view of a girl being pushed from the wings into a spotlight which drags her forward, into the light cage. Whiteness drifts over the first few rows, which are empty.

Belle covers her face. The music pumps. Belle splays her fingers. There is a commotion under the music. The three lads clamber to the front row, bright in their Hawaiian shirts. Belle sits up straight to see the girl bat her sequinned lashes as her fixed glitter smile is taken wider by a real one.

'Go for it!' the lads enthuse.

Triumphant in her light cage, the girl's back is still arched, her chest thrust and her legs splayed, but she doesn't look pantomime crude any more.

Belle's fingers are pushing as if to get rid of the cowl, which has suddenly become claustrophobic as the girl turns and teases with receding hips. The lads oblige with calls for her to come back. But instead she bends and grins clownishly from between her legs. They laugh. She slips the bra straps off and twists to face them. Just her palms hold the skimpy remains of her costume in place.

The girl was nothing special when she came on. She's got the whole audience wriggling.

Flesh squeezes out and out, until finally, with a flourish, the light cage girl throws away her brassiere.

The velour chair arm between Belle and Sylvie is all that's left of social niceties – and it is thin. They are generating so much heat they're at risk of fusing. The front row applauds uproariously.

'BRAVO!' There's whistling and shouting. 'MORE!'

The girl bows and blows the lads a hearty kiss. The pleasure was all hers.

After the show, outside, Belle and Sylvie find their gazes can't meet but go skidding and bouncing off each other's like same poles of magnets. Standing side by side, backs to a wall, it seems their lungs have filled so thoroughly with the cold of Xanadu's auditorium that they can't cope with a more neutral temperature. Breathing is fast and shallow.

For the centre of town, it is empty. The street has been cleared of market detritus. A drunk sways towards the brick cradle horizon. The midnight atmosphere is sweet with smells of baking bread. A cat howls over the rooftops.

Sylvie's skirt-suit is still shaped to fit a shop-hanger, disagreeing with her body. She rips the jacket off to reveal a T-shirt that has a pink love-heart on the front. She turns her hair into a pony-tail with a jolly toggle and Belle feels as protective towards her as if she was a kid sister.

'Have you got somewhere to stay?'

'Of *course*.' Sylvie's mother would die if she knew she'd booked into a hostel.

'All right, is it?'

Sylvie had to wash the hand-basin before she could wash herself. 'It's fine.'

'Which way are you going?'

'Which way are you?'

'Fancy a drink? I know a late-night bar we could stop off at.'

'I wouldn't mind a cup of tea.'

Belle hesitates. 'How about round to mine, then?'

Sylvie's father told her never to trust strangers. Her mother told her to trust her instincts. 'That'd be lovely.'

Clover Court offers some illusions. A 1930s' block, its combination of curved sides and deck-flat roof can launch it as a cruise-ship through the imagination, if the viewer is distant. Close up, it is a dilapidated building, particularly gloomy after dark when street-light fingered into cracks in the façade casts gaping shadows. The communal door swings off its hinges. Rubbish has blown in and collected at the edges of the stairwell.

Slowed already, Sylvie stops completely. 'I didn't know it'd be so far.'

'Only five tube stops.'

'And a ten-minute walk either end.'

'You're here now.' Belle urges, 'Go on. Second floor.'

The lights are faulty. Sylvie sighs then ascends in dashes that coincide with the fluorescent buzzing. Belle's voice echoes.

'It's the first on your right.'

For Sylvie, home is a castle of the heritage kind, front porch kept immaculate in case of visitors. The central glass panel of the entrance to number 12 is reinforced not only with wire mesh but also bars. There isn't even a welcome mat.

'You're having me on.'

Belle's hands in her pockets splay her jacket apologetically. As long as no one she knew saw it, she could convince herself that home was a place that didn't matter. She comes in, goes out, sleeps a bit and maybe defecates in between. When she first moved here, she had a locksmith fit hinge bolts and a London bar and refrained from three mortises only because he told her that that many would weaken the frame. She said, 'Better safe than sorry.' He shook his head even as he was adding up the bill. There is so much metal the wood can't breathe. Belle has to grasp the letterbox and pull it more tightly shut – pin-stripes taut across her back – before she can shoulder-barge her door free of its fortifications.

She often forgets to throw the carrier bag of rubbish out before she leaves. The heat and smell build up. Belle and Sylvie flatten themselves, faces pinched, as a trapped day's worth rushes past.

Now is Sylvie's last chance to make a run for it. Belle hangs her head. Sylvie peeks hers round.

Belle is overjoyed. Sylvie's smile is faint but there.

'Front room?'

'Kitchen.'

'Is it all yours then?'

'Rented.'

'But you live in it on your own, do you? Two bed, is it?'

Belle nods. Sylvie looks round crossly.

The hall's bleak – bare boards extending to a cluster of half-open doors that offer glimpses of a skull-like fireplace, of just enough watery blue to drown in – but the kitchen is worse, as cramped as a coffin without the nailed-in security. There is hardly room to breathe yet because it has no linking surfaces there are dark spaces everywhere, between the Formica-topped fridge and ancient cooker, under the sink, above the wall-cupboard that juts out at head height, behind its precariously stacked odds and sods contents.

Even Sylvie's simple act of moving things aside to reach the mugs makes the cupboard's contents look more organised. The teapot is chipped and cracked. She wraps a tea-towel round it as a cosy. Steam rises from the mugs between them on the table.

Belle leans forward, eyes wide. 'Did you and your friends used to lie on each other's beds of a Saturday afternoon and read out extracts from *Jackie* magazines?'

The love-heart on Sylvie's T-shirt seems to swell at the mention of her upbringing. She squashes dried-milk granules against the side of her mug with a teaspoon. 'We read *Brides* mostly.'

Belle is an ungainly mess sprawling from shoulder blades hooked over the chair-back. Sylvie is a picture of cross-legged elegance. She has already noticed the Harrods label inside Belle's jacket and sifted the plumminess from her accent. Looking at the leaflets fanning out from the noticeboard stuck behind the kitchen door, she wonders, 'What are they for, then? Concerts, readings, things like that?'

Belle clasps her palm over her mug so tightly that she appears to have stopped it steaming. Her mouth curves into a very open smile. Her eyes are the clearest blue. 'Sure,' she says, tilting her chair so, as part of a casual rocking motion on its back legs, she can push the leaflets promoting Lilian White further into the Bermuda triangle created by the opened door. From the pine-framed noticeboard her mother is smiling, listening, laughing into a corner that contains a mop and bucket.

Belle bites a nail and rips it to the quick. Blood leaks from the corner. She staunches it on her shirt cuff. The weave soaks it, criss-crossing red immediately over the white.

Party sounds float through the window and laugh up to the ceiling. The grimy strip-light casing is a leafy canopy, dappling Belle and Sylvie beneath. The checked table-top is a picnic cloth spread between them. They are physical negatives of each other, one a blue-eyed brunette of a mannish build, the other a brown-eyed blonde with a classic pear-shaped figure.

Their fingers are close, Belle's gnawed, evidently in need of attention, Sylvie's plumply manicured and clearly capable of giving it.

And the dominoes that got knocked when Belle first phoned Xanadu's keep on knocking and again Belle acts on impulse.

Sylvie catches a laugh in her hand, eyes bashful over the top.

She can't move in literally now. Her suitcase is still at the hostel.

On her way out, she picks up Belle's carrier bag of rubbish. Handles neatly tied, it is a little snow-white Santa sack, the gift of it that it is being taken away.

'I'll put it in a bin,' says Sylvie.

'Thanks.'

As Belle shuts the door behind her, she seems to be flattened to it by the force of Sylvie leaving. Her cheeks are flushed. Her eyes dart. She can't work out if she's more pleased at having made such a connection with someone that they're prepared to move in, or dismayed that Sylvie saw the state she lives in, or angry at the possibility that Sylvie might consider herself above Belle and in a position to judge her when she does come back. *If.* Belle panics. That would be worse for her, far worse, if Sylvie didn't come back. Looking round, she thinks what the quickest difference is she can make.

Lilian must have put her on the show's mailing list. Franked envelopes keep coming through the letterbox and, naturally, respectfully, Belle pins them up. It hadn't struck her as odd to have accumulated so many before Sylvie came round and saw.

Standing at the noticeboard in the kitchen, Belle takes one promotional leaflet down, assuring herself that it's not that she wants to throw any of them away, since, even if it's only indirectly, they are gifts from her mother. But now she sees that she'd made a shrine. And not to Lilian in general but to her success. There's nothing personal up there on the board, no letters, no snapshot photos – not that Belle has many in the first place. Lilian is not keen on casual things like that.

Why write – Lilian thinks – when mother and daughter live in the same city? And how can someone in her profession feel comfortable with snapshots? Her image is her work.

But, whatever the reason for its imbalance, Belle concludes that the display of Lilian memorabilia, and the way it dominates her kitchen, must have looked weird to Sylvie – and now she sees the extent of it, it begins to feel weird to Belle – and anyway, many of the leaflets' edges are curling and going brown.

From every PR photo, Lilian's full attention is on the viewer. Belle starts at the bottom, pulling down the images one after another, warily at first – the gaze stays flatly smiling – then more quickly until drawing pins are flying out like bullets.

The board is empty. Belle stands back, but instead of feeling even a bit satisfied, she is overwhelmed by how much she has failed to do to her flat, by how thoroughly it has rejected her – refusing to let her choice of paint or lino stick, creeping mould into her water biscuits, souring even her refrigerated milk.

Just as she does every night, Belle knows she will end up to-ing and fro-ing through the small hours, twizzling her hair, dragging the duvet, a massive comfort blanket curling and slapping the dust from the floorboards behind her like a bloated wedding train, back, and forth, back, forth.

She thinks she may as well start in her bedroom, lying on the bed in the launderette-grey cover, eyes wide open. It doesn't matter how late it is. Unless she's blind drunk, sleep evades her and all she can do is stare at the ceiling. Tonight it is quaking with the sounds of the couple upstairs having sex.

Belle block her ears, sits, collapses, twists to her stomach and onto her back again. A single feather rises. She spreads her legs. Sweat creeps towards her pubic hair. She could feel more aroused if she was manipulating her clitoris with a handful of fishfingers. She sighs.

She did her sexual maturing as if she was on a crammer course – at discos checking the luminescent hands of her watch before wrestling some boy into position, his hand under her bra, her hand down his pants, whatever was due to be crossed off her mental check-list next. She thought she had by-passed teenage and gone straight to adult but somehow she found herself instead in a wilderness. It should have been well charted.

Belle had seen sex dissected so intimately on TV and in films that sometimes she could almost see the screen directions scrolling up the wall.

Pant louder. Moan.

She became conscious of not bending forwards on top because it was an unflattering angle for her breasts, which swung, thin dugs. And fellatio could get noisy enough to make her want to yell, 'Cut!' and take the shot again.

If love could have come, she missed it worrying about the script and about the end, which she wanted to be sure to arrive at with some dignity. So she never let anyone drag on longer than an affair. But she couldn't necessarily enjoy the one-night stands either.

She thinks of Zone Fantastica and suddenly her insides are screeching as if some crucial part has gone missing, a lynch-pin, and without it she might fly apart. She clutches herself. Yet, the Xanadu girls did perfectly well without their lynch-pins. Indeed, they were strengthened, so confident to be out that they were laughing, able also to be on the street in posters, demarcated so absolutely that they could be cut and pasted anywhere and still be the same, polished to a Vaseline shine.

Belle is practically running to her bathroom. The high small window goes deep through the wall to capture the moon. She jams a Bic razor and a bar of soap on the ledge.

In the tub, if she tiptoes, she can see her pubic hair in the cabinet mirror. It is currently bushy, which obviously won't do, she realises, shaking her head. She will have to have a neat topiary line if she is to fit those G-strings.

The first cut brings up a large, curiously romantic lock of hair. She leans across to break it under the sink's cold tap. The cabinet still reflects a froth of white. She slices through the other corner and washes this evidence too down the sink.

She drops carefully to her knees. Water rises between her thighs, gradually lifting the hair-specked foam, which breaks up and floats away. As she stands she bites her lip.

It's not that she is averse to getting rid of excess. But she has had a triangle between her legs for a long time. It's a shock to her to see a mole that has been hidden since she was a child.

In the mirror, the front elevation shows her pubes as a black slit. Looking down, a mohican sticks out, thin but dense.

With small, curved nail scissors she snips the top off. It seems strange to have removed so much then to stop.

The remaining hair is her pudenda's exclamation mark of adulthood.

*

Back in bed, when Belle does finally drift off, it is such a surprise that she seems to retain consciousness.

She is looking for the shoe box she used to keep her action men in. The search is anguished, between outsized sofa and impossibly far-away oriental vase – which threatens to fall and break so Belle must save it and is further delayed.

Only she and the action men know how much they mean to her. But the guilt in case Lilian should find out has always been enormous. And so of course when Belle does see the box, miraculously in the middle of the vast room, tied prettily with pink ribbon, she can't be fast enough and dives to grasp it. Her relief to hear it rattle is so great that, sobbing, she embraces the box. But then there is a simple sound of sawing. They are action men. Their job is to get out. And as they do their plastic mouths are smirking and they are scrambling across the floor in different directions and she is turning every which way, calling, 'Don't go, please, not again!'

She does manage to grab just one. With both his plastic hands, he takes hold of her thumb and bites. That it is physical pain makes her almost glad. Except the teeth marks form a crescent moon that is thinning already and will soon also disappear.

He shakes his plastic head, apparently disappointed.

'Why can't you understand? It's nothing personal.'

chapter 2

*E*ven while she was growing up there, Lilian's place always felt mysterious to Belle. The fact that it was an apartment suggested other apartments, yet there never seemed to be anyone else around. Lilian had converted the top floor of a warehouse. She was ahead of her time. Belle's schoolmates all lived in traditional homes. Although she did think it might be nice to have a cosy   as opposed to machine-sized – living room, Belle became glad to be different.

She would sit at the window and gaze out over the industrial landscape. It had an unsettling beauty. The colours – crumbling brick, rusted scaffolding – were a permanent sunset. And when the sun was actually setting, windows blazed, making the surrounding buildings infernos. Young Belle pressed her hands flat to the cold window pane.

In fact, the area wasn't a total wasteland. There were several estates nearby, turn-of-the-century low-rises full of people, who all used local facilities. The pub, it was understood between Lilian and Belle, was trashy. To the owners of a washing machine and dryer, the launderette was redundant. But Belle did sneak to the corner shop, to waste her pocket-money on sweets. It was a place Lilian particularly disliked, feeling sure that behind the stacks of groceries, small-talk festered.

Belle would creep up the worn stone front steps. Inside the door, she would covet packet jellies and tins of custard powder, vanilla essence and HP Sauce, and slip a finger round the tin of a Fray Bentos pie. Then, at the counter, she would stand on a milk-crate and lean her elbow by the till in a most adult fashion.

The shopkeeper took to her. He had a lot of grey hair and a big smile and he never once hurried her. They talked about how too many pear-drops cut the tongue but at least don't stick in the teeth like fruit gums. The shopkeeper sometimes ventured on to the weather, but never asked anything tricksy. Belle could leave with bags of All Sorts and a clear conscience. Except once. She had been trying to include another regular customer in her discussion on sherbet fountains.

'Out on your own a lot, aren't you, doll?' they had responded. 'Latch-key kid, then, are you?'

From then on, Belle preferred to snack in the quiet of her mother's kitchen on wholesome 'Lite' Ryvitas.

She travelled to school. She went away for holidays and elsewhere to be babysat. It was easy to enter a state of defensive isolation.

What were neighbours for? They were people to borrow cups of sugar from. Belle didn't take sugar.

Anyway, Lilian's apartment was special. It was all illusions. The living area was as expansive as a sunny wheatfield.
The brick wall at the far end had as its centre a wooden door
that opened horizontally down, lowered by chains. But the
drawbridge was to thin air. Its original cast-iron winch was
still in place but now holding baskets of flowers. This was a
goods entrance. No goods would be arriving. Lilian had
everything inside arranged immaculately.

The living area was an artful mix of antique and modern
furniture. Belle tended to curl up on the rug rather than the
sofa because otherwise she could never get the scatter cushions looking elegantly casual again. The high-backed
broganza chair was Belle's magical hide-out, the space
beneath the trestle table a lion's lair.

Belle calculated that the living area was between 110 and
140 jetés from one end to the other. This made her mother's
room awfully distant. It was a treat for her to get to spend
time in there with Lilian, which happened, for example,
early evening if Lilian had a date. She would let her daughter help her to prepare.

On one particular occasion, Lilian was also sorting
through her wardrobe. She had heaped all the definite
rejects on the bed. Her preference was for tactile fabrics.
Eleven-year-old Belle crawled into lace, velvet, silk, swathing
herself in softness and Lilian's scent. She shut her eyes and
kicked her legs in the air.

Beside the wardrobe, Lilian pushed her blouse sleeves
higher.

'You are lovely, you are fine,' Belle chanted. 'You really
are, superior to wine!'

'Doesn't *quite* scan, darling,' Lilian said, inspecting a cashmere sweater.

'I made that up, on the spot!' Belle declared, leaping to trampoline her triumph.

'Not on the bed.' Lilian held up a mink stole. 'What do you think – too "matronly"?'

'You'll *never* look old,' Belle promised and dropped into a crêpe-de-Chine gown. She stuffed a couple of scarves to fill the bust. Her mother was experimenting with the veil of a pill-box hat, seducing herself through the mirror.

'Lilian,' Belle said casually, and again, drawing the word out, 'Lil-lian.'

Her mother tossed the hat in Belle's direction. 'Yes?'

'I was just wondering. How much longer do you think I'll be, well, you know, *flat-chested*?'

Lilian laughed. 'I'm sorry, darling. I only wish my worries were so small.'

Belle pulled the hat over her face as a mask. Her blush crept past the edges.

'Anyhow,' Lilian said as she checked a zip, 'you'll look fine whether you're a D cup or a double-A.' Suddenly her voice was hard. 'Although, you could do something about your posture,' as if her daughter was gawky out of spite. 'Why on earth,' she muttered absently, caftan in one hand, pair of ski-pants in the other, 'did I keep these?'

Belle's voice was restrained by the hat. 'Lilian, may I ask you something?'

'Of course, darling,' giving a taffeta skirt a shake.

Belle stuck her fingers into the hat's veil and pulled it out of shape. 'You know when you were at college' – she had all Lilian's attention now – 'just before I was born . . .'

'Do you think I should donate to Oxfam or Children in Need?'

Belle repositioned her elbows so her shoulder blades looked mutated. 'Whatever you think best.'

Fists rapping opposite elbows, Lilian double-checked. 'Did you want to ask me something?'

So quietly that her breath didn't disturb the feathers of the boa in front of her mouth, Belle murmured, 'No.'

Struck by a magnificent idea, Lilian threw her arms in the air. She swept over and pressed a camisole to her daughter. 'Naturally, I'm obliged to give to charity.' She winked. 'But you can choose a few things first.'

Belle pushed the camisole off and sat up. Lilian drew closer still. The mattress was well sprung. The dents their bodies made stayed separate. Lilian's voice agitated the hairs on the back of Belle's neck. 'I thought you might like to try flute lessons next. You'll make a charming flautist.'

Still hunched, Belle said, 'Thank you very much.'

'Now.' Getting Lilian ready for dinners was good, parties were next best, and dates were most exciting of all. 'Help me choose my outfit.' Belle's advice was crucial.

'The platinum dress,' she cried. She hopped from foot to foot. 'Wear the platinum tendril dress!'

'All right,' Lilian conceded as she plumped her old clothes into smaller, more manageable mounds. 'Go and get some bin-liners from the drawer by the kitchen sink.' Belle rolled her eyes. She knew where they kept the cleaning equipment.

Lilian only ever let Belle see her nude when she was

feeling in top-notch condition. Today she was premenstrual, a little bloated.

Belle left the room long enough for her to at least partially change and position herself at the dressing-table mirror. By the time Belle had finished bagging rejected outfits, Lilian had cleansed and was re-applying foundation.

Perched on the edge of the bed, Belle thought how she could get a bra and stuff it with cotton wool if necessary to make herself look the part. But the more she saw Lilian preparing, awed by the overall impression, the more elusive the essence of femininity seemed to her, partly because Lilian had such a firm grip on it. Belle tried to concentrate on specifics, to isolate techniques.

In the mirror, her mother's reflection tilted its head back. Belle's hands shot out instinctively as if to catch her should she fall. Lilian swept shadow into her sockets.

'Why,' Belle asked, 'do you use a brush for the eyeshadow, not a cotton bud?'

'You funny thing,' Lilian said, and bared her teeth as if her daughter was so delicious she could eat her.

'But *why*?'

'Because.' In the mirror, Lilian stretched her mouth.

Belle stretched hers too. 'And 'ot a'out 'at?'

Lilian lowered the scarlet lip pencil. Her lips, lined not filled yet, looked very thin. 'What, darling?'

Time was ticking on.

'Why don't you skip the liner and just put lipstick on, on its own?' Belle's voice wavered. 'I don't understand.'

'The pencil acts as a seal,' Lilian said. 'Without it, there's leakage. Definition blurs.'

Her reflection, distant, was doll-perfect. Lilian twisted out lipstick, an obscene, curled tongue.

'Who's your date with?' Belle demanded.

'You'll see.' With a big smile she asked, 'Will you zip me up?'

The platinum dress was a tight fit. Belle had to brace a hand in the small of Lilian's back.

Lilian was patient. Belle fiddled and twisted, arranging the tendrils between Lilian's shoulder blades. Lilian couldn't see to correct or advise. Her mother would spend the whole evening wearing Belle's decisions. Belle felt elated.

'There. You're ready.'

To be sure Lilian looked absolutely magnificent, Belle ran a quick circle.

'Why can't you just *walk* occasionally,' Lilian snapped.

The buzzer sounded. Lilian held Belle's shoulders so tight her daughter was lifted slightly off her feet.

'You answer it.'

'OK,' Belle reassured.

Lilian's love interests, especially when they were would-be or has-been boyfriends, were their secret joke. Belle puffed her chest as she crossed the living area. Hand on the latch, she prepared a patronising look. She pulled the door open.

It was Geoffrey, looking about as sophisticated as a grizzly bear in a tuxedo. She giggled. He didn't usually go to this trouble just for picking her up to take her back to his place to be babysat.

'Didn't she tell you?'

'Tell me what?' Belle asked and took his hand.

Geoffrey took it back. He stared at his big, shuffling feet. 'I'm here for Lilian. Tonight it's me. I'm her date.'

Geoffrey Thomas has known Lilian since childhood. His parents were stationed overseas. When he wasn't boarding, Lilian's parents regularly took him in at the Knoll. He appears once in almost all their photograph albums, his characteristic round wire glasses framing a serious expression softened by hair that has grown still more unruly as the years progress and whiter, as if absorbing the clouds of stone he creates in his work, carving sun-dials for cash and sculpture for himself. He does sell his own work, just not enough to make a living. He decided it was unfair to impose an austerity he'd chosen on anyone else and he resisted the urge to replicate himself through children. Belle is practically a niece to him. For relaxation he tends to go to exhibitions or read books that relate to themes he is exploring in his work. He has been glad of her function as an excuse to do things like making chocolate krispies or kite-flying on Primrose Hill. In return, even when he has been forced from his studio, from his own work, he always takes care to stay attentive if she's edgy, as she is on his doorstep today.

Quickly wiping off mascara with the back of her hand, Belle holds up tropical fruit drink and a be-ribboned cake-box as Geoffrey's door opens.

Goggles pushed onto his forehead, the clean shape they have left is the only bit of him not covered in white dust, which is still settling, blurring, making him seem far away. While he fits his glasses on with one hand, Geoffrey puts the other on her shoulder.

'Belle! A month gone already?'

'I come too often.'

'You're very good to me.'

She shuffles. 'You'd never have breaks otherwise, and anyway,' she says, suddenly pushing past him into his hall, 'it's not only for your benefit. Where are we eating?'

'Wherever you fancy. Kitchen?'

'Terrace.'

He's still shutting the door as she's running up the stairs.

Belle's block also has a flat roof that would be perfect for sitting out on, say, with a towel for sunbathing or a chair and a magazine. No one else does. Belle's convinced that if she presumed to, one of the other tenants would be bound to go up to fix their aerial and catch her. So she finds Geoffrey's a haven. His house is remote from people anyway. The railway bridge on one side and factory on the other are redundant now except as supports, generating weed fingers to help hold his building upright. Its walls rise to give a solid back and an open outlook to the roof terrace. His pots and baskets contain mainly fresh herbs or powerfully scented flowers such as honeysuckle. Although, if an interesting weed starts growing, he will encourage it.

Belle opens out a deckchair. Feet up on the parapet, torso swooping with the line of the canvas, she looks her full length, and feels it too – indeed, she's chuckling to be so immediately and totally relaxed. She breaks into laughter that takes her whole body with it, her arms and legs wildly up, and only coming squarely down in the deckchair just before merriment creases out from her eyes.

'Did I miss something?'

'Just glad to be here.'

Geoffrey is in the middle of a firing. He sits on a straight-back. Belle fixes a playful frown on the chisel he's still turning in his hands as she curls the cake-box ribbon.

'OK, OK.' He puts the chisel in his pocket and she's ripping the box open.

'I didn't get anything with cream in case it went off. Florentine, Danish, apricot or apple tart?' she demands. 'Well? Which one, or two?'

He shrugs crossly. 'And I suppose you always eat like this.'

'Of course!'

'Then why are you so thin?'

'Just built this way.'

'You weren't last time. It's not clever to starve yourself, you know.'

'What do you care? You're not my—' Head flailing, her eyes flick to the escapist aspects of his roof. 'You're my favourite ingrate, as it happens; I turn up with cakes and what do I get for it?' She lurches suddenly as if to chuck the box over the parapet. 'If you don't want them . . .'

'I want!' he obliges, but he is beginning to be transported by how much she looks like Lilian did at her age, the clear blue of her eyes in such contrast to her black hair that it seems one or other of them must be false. He takes off his glasses and squeezes the bridge of his nose. 'What do *you* want?'

'I'm here because you need a break, remember?' She slaps her thigh and imitates a hearty laugh. 'Why did the chicken cross the road? To get to the other side. Come on, you always used to like that one; we'd laugh together till it hurt. How many giraffes can you fit in a mini? It depends . . .'

'. . . how many elephants you put in first.'

He turns his spectacles over in his hand. 'Is it boyfriend trouble?'

Belle snorts. 'If only!'

'Job?'

Belle asks melodramatically, 'Which one?'

'Lilian?'

'Of course not.'

They both stare at the flat surface of the roof terrace, which seems to be leaking Tarmac at the edges. Belle picks at a scab on her knee.

Pointing at the cake-box, he says, 'You don't have to bribe me. If you want to tell me something I'll listen; ask anything, just go ahead – I know Lilian's not good at talking. Don't forget she's a different generation.'

'Only the same as you.' But she's hunched now in the deckchair, watching Geoffrey float from her into memories.

'It started so magnificently for her – plum job in "the metropolis", as she liked to call it; lodgings with a couple of girl friends.' His fingers rise as if to touch the things that he's describing – 'piano in the front room, dozens of cocktail shakers. They threw parties constantly. I think she invited me to every one of her "swinging do's", which was kind.' He frowns. 'It seemed every man she met fell in love with her.'

Her voice is coaxing. 'I'm sure she loved you most.'

He stares right at her, shocked, almost hopeful. He puts his head in his hands. 'I filled a gap.'

The creases in his forehead deepen as if to get to the pertinent facts. 'I think it was seeing Marjory give up her career that did it.' Amazed, he tallies the years on his fingers. 'So recently, and just because Marjory and her fiancé worked together at the network, if she wanted to marry she had to leave. And she did. Perhaps Lilian felt betrayed seeing her best friend become "just a housewife".' He shrugs. 'Anyway, come what may she wasn't going to make the same mistake herself.' He can't help laughing. 'She was always rotten about her mother, saying she "smothered her intelligence" – killed her independence with terries, she said, and then Lilian made her do it all over again when . . .' he briefly sees and seems annoyed by Belle's presence.

She's got the scab off her knee completely now. It was almost healed.

It is true that she hasn't heard every detail before but then she has always accepted that most of them don't matter. She knows Lilian was brave and that Belle is lucky – and she is grateful. Geoffrey is trampling about in gaps she doesn't want to be filled. She digs into flesh.

'Mind, she couldn't have coped herself.'

'But how are *you*?' Belle murmurs.

'By then she was ill, although she'd never have admitted it herself.' He is becoming angry. '*I* told her, her mother told her.'

Lilian's arms slipped to nothing. The thickening at her waist only made her more determined.

'She dieted constantly. She was dangerously thin. When she knew for sure, she was nearly seven months gone.'

He jams his thumb and forefinger under his glasses into his eyes. She never bloomed. She looked as if the foetus was killing her.

Then Geoffrey seems bemused. 'Menstruation can simply stop if a woman's badly underweight, can't it?' looking directly at Belle for confirmation. 'There probably was no significant "missed period", was there?'

She wouldn't even talk about menstruating, just left out a packet of sanitary towels, so how, thinks Belle, would she know? – and she kicks her ankles, eroding rhythmically.

If she doesn't answer, she thinks he must stop.

Geoffrey is tired – of having been in love for so long, of having taken on so much emotional responsibility for the daughter of his object of desire.

'Her contract was flexible,' he notes. 'She convalesced at her parents'. Mrs George adored the baby.'

Belle flinches to be referred to as 'the baby'.

'You were only with your grandparents through most of the difficult first year, maybe two,' he rounds up impatiently. 'As you know already, you weren't planned. But you were very much wanted. Lilian nursed you as much as her schedule allowed. She spent a fortune on nannies.' He leans close. He grips Belle's shoulder, squeezing his words into her. 'She loves you very much indeed.'

That's all Belle needs to know, isn't it, what she came to hear, he thinks, that she's loved?

Belle is staring at the palms of her hands as if the lines on them have been erased. Her mother is all Geoffrey seems able to talk to her about; her grandfather mistakes her for Lilian completely.

Belle is cross suddenly. The walls of his terrace are a trap.

The yard below is covered with corrugated plastic. Dark shapes jut beneath like pillars.

She has seen his sundials, but never his sculptures. That he's a doer and a shaper is the part of himself he keeps from her.

'When are you going to show me your work?'

He is keen to get back to it. 'What about yours?' His face is in hers. 'For Christ's sake! A bit of filing and typing won't kill you. Just stick at a job for once!'

She pulls back into shadow. Perhaps Geoffrey could be shocked out of his studio, even mid-sculpting, if he found out about Xanadu's.

Lilian stuck at her job. She is a big success. Her dressing room is fragrant with bouquets. Her name is on the door.

She sits stiffly, hair scraped back. Tonight the mirror's bulbs are particularly unkind – her face looks parched.

She has thirty minutes to prepare. A couple of publicity shots exuding glamour are propped on her dressing table, reminders of how she will look. She tightens her robe. Newspaper cuttings stuck up round her mirror confirm critical and popular acclaim.

The more she gets the more she needs. Without recognition she is nothing. But the public recognition can never be of her private face, which she hardly dares see herself.

Her case of cosmetics extends to three levels. She obscures a section of face with her hand as she draws powder to her eyelid's edge, exaggerating its size. She hollows her cheeks. She plumps her mouth.

Lilian bows her head. She is famous in a profession Geoffrey once described as vacuous. She laughed, then proceeded to list her most impressive upcoming guests. It is barbed consolation that she is a mouthpiece for activists, biologists, composers – it doesn't matter who they are: on her show, to talk to the nation, or at least 0.8% of it, they have to go through Lilian White. They can look at her. She is mediator. Only Lilian White can address the camera directly, in close-up, her eyes meeting the viewers' in their living rooms.

In front of her dressing-room mirror, she dusts gold highlights. In the corridor outside, the PA is braced. The director Oliver Bradwell strides over. He tells his PA, 'You're needed on set.'

The PA looks relieved.

'I'll see to Lilian.'

Oliver is a floppily tall man who likes a laugh and designer clothing. Lilian favours suitors who have academic weight. He hadn't even considered her, until he found out that she had a child. He became curious There must be a soft side to her.

Inside, Lilian looks at her watch and frowns. She usually takes her nerves out on the PA. Oliver pops his head round her dressing-room door.

'Fifteen minutes,' he announces.

Lilian's smile is forced so quickly it is a grimace. Amused, he rests his head against the top of the doorframe, as if to emphasise that he is looking down on her. It may be a highbrow version, but hers is just another pretty face.

*

Xanadu's foyer feels oppressive with no one else in it. The maroon walls, distantly velvety at night, are clearly visible now, sparking round the worn patches. Unevenness brings them in like cave walls, thrusting the pictures closer: nearly nude girl – girl – girl. They are designed to represent a variety of fantasies. Some of the headdresses are bigger than others. The items round the wrists, ankles and groin vary in materials – chain, lace, leather – but they all cover roughly the same, small surface area. Belle is in front of a lightbox in which a woman is wrapped around a monster gear-stick, her bare arse thrust towards her ear just by the suggestion of what her fingers are doing to the chrome shaft between her legs. The image curves perfectly, smoothly. Belle still can't believe it, but if she has a job here, she must have a physique others will aspire to as well.

Standing back, she wipes the accumulation of liner from the corners of her eyes and stares at the trails of mucus and chemicals on her fingertips, momentarily confused. Then she rubs them into the underside of her hem.

There is something angelic about Sylvie. Belle imagines her into the lightbox. Even blonde pubes won't differentiate her, since they will have been depilated.

Sylvie has a face that fits in anywhere. In the middle of the stage, in the middle of a group of girls, she wears the smile that is easy to ignore. The girls whisper and touch each other. Hands neat in her white-ski-panted lap, perched cross-legged on her suitcase, Sylvie waits.

She always aligns herself with someone who will absorb all the attention. Belle, it seems, can't breathe without stumbling or knocking something over. Beside her, Sylvie should be able to slip through unnoticed. She stares around her keenly.

Brightly lit for rehearsal, the auditorium has a midday feel to it. The seats undulate in the distance, a landscape of vermillion poppies. The stage is a platform, the assortment of props on it adding to the railway station atmosphere. The straps and clips on the set of outsize bongo drums make them look in transit. The elevator suggests other levels of departure.

Except there's a pervading quiet. A cart ready to be filled with baggage has fallen at an angle. By a small door on a wall a piece of paper the breadth of a timetable is blank. It is as if trains don't stop here any more but by some strange, huge administrative error; there has been no general announcement and the passengers who do know are too embarrassed to tell the others.

At the back, sitting with their knees up, foreheads touching, Sue and Cheryl apply unnecessary concentration to doing each other's toenails, their toes spread with wads of cotton wool.

'*Fuchsia*. Nice,' Sue murmurs, brushing varnish so slowly that she rakes in a tremor.

Cheryl had once imagined herself in a Cameron Mackintosh production. Sue would have been happy with panto. They have been here on and off for seven and five years respectively.

But the Xanadu hours allow them to keep on trying. There is always the possibility of *that lucky break*. Debs and Imo, lying either side of Sylvie's travel bag, seem elevated slightly by the chance of it. Girls who get in from the porn side of the industry are lead weights.

In a lime green waistcoat, cerise leggings and leopard-skin ankle boots, Mae Monroe stands on the apron of the stage, hands on her hips. A defiant stance generally has the chin up, inviting someone to just dare try and strike it. She doesn't even need that suggestion of interaction. Her chin is where it should be to keep her wholly balanced.

She has done dirty-mixing. Now she has paid off most of the mortgage on her Streatham one-bed. And actually, her gig's been mainly pubs. She only filled in at Peepland as a favour for a friend. She is 26 and planning to grow old a bit more gracefully.

Like sand marked by a tide, the way the others lie behind her appears to have been dictated by her presence.

Belle is at the top of the stairs, about to enter the auditorium, the doors open behind her like wings. Underarm hair sticking out of her sleeveless dress draws attention to the butch wideness of her shoulders. Her waist is slinky Lycra. Her footless tights are still more diminutive, tapering to sandals big and hard enough to kick somebody's head in.

On stage, some of the girls are limbering up already. One hasn't even bothered to take her coat off yet, doing pliés in a windbreaker. Nearby, a few girls are in a circle, hands placed on backs in front, legs raised high, leaving stiletto, bovver boot, plimsoll serene in limbo.

There are no clocks, no windows in the auditorium. Belle twists her watch to her wrist's underside. Geoffrey's may not have been the haven she'd imagined, but this place, she thinks, is even better, even more remote.

At the front of the stage, Mae Monroe in particular is so centred that it's almost possible to see a plumb-line going through her to the core of the earth. She might get knocked and spin a bit but she would soon settle back to how she is, with the same slightly amused set of her mouth, one green eye permanently critical.

Belle leaps on stage with a huge grin, grabs Mae's hand and is shaking vigorously. '*Very* pleased to meet you. I'm new as well, as a matter of fact. I mean, you must be wondering how I know you only just started as well.' Belle clumps closer, explaining, 'I saw you yesterday, outside . . .'

Suddenly it's Mae who's shaking Belle's hand till her arm's almost taken from its socket. 'Pleased to meet you too!'

Belle persists, 'I recognise you from outside Pee—'

'The name's Mae,' she almost shouts. 'Mae Monroe.'

She has no secrets, but there are orders for facts to come out in that are preferable, and Peepland is one she hopes they don't all know about yet. Belle shifts about.

'Like the image,' Mae says drily. 'Audrey Hepburn with undcrarm hair. Nice.'

'Thanks,' says Belle, twisting her hands.

Mae's face, once quite heavily acned, looks not scarred but translucent. She blows her gum. Pinkness from inside her emerges, soft yet taut, prepared to burst. Belle moves closer. Mae lets her.

New girls generally expect Ricky Vincent to come through the same entrance the punters will, from the side. At the back of the auditorium, he scrambles up from the fire exit and strides down the aisle towards the stage.

A chubby peacock of a man, today he is dressed in satin and denim, chest puffed into his shiny blue shirt, neat fingers hooked into his belt. His shoes are shined enough to reflect the bum fluff of his chin.

The auditorium is immediately silent, no scuffling, not a single cough. The plaster sky is heavy. While girls huddle to the middle of the stage in the glare, Ricky slips under the bellies of the spotlights, perfectly positioned to be shady yet with the capacity to dazzle. His shoes and shirt catch light and send it out in shafts if he moves. Girls squint. Around his dark, small shape, rows and rows of empty seats radiate. He has velveteen authority behind him, they a pock-marked wall.

Sylvie moves closer to Belle who moves closer to Mae. ''Ere!', 'Watch it!', 'Gerroff m'foot!' – cries of protest flying up and down sew the group more tightly together, into one huge generic girl with lots of different types of shoes.

Just the sight of him has made Belle's insides curdle. And, conscious that her outside is made up of shoulder blades that jut out one wrong way and stomach another under saggy boobs, arms crossed, she glances side to side. Debs is picking wax out of her ears. Imo lets slip bits of a tune she's playing in her head.

'Here at Xanadu's,' Ricky Vincent finally begins, teeth flashing from his silhouette, 'we represent a long and fine tradition. It's glamorous, it's fast, it's bizarre; it's erotic not pornographic. Striptease is an *art*.' His hands are as white as a magician's gloves. They touch his heart. 'Nothing gives the same inner emotion as seeing a nude body, which is *the* most beautiful machine, in the *universe*.'

'Here here,' murmurs Sylvie.

'Ha ha,' mutters Debs.

'*And*,' Ricky Vincent says more loudly, 'one of the things that keeps us above the rest at Xanadu's is our emphasis on *content*. It is not' – giving Mae a look – '*not* just Tits and Ass' – turning to Sylvie – 'and this season, the theme is "Our Royal Heritage".'

'How are we going to celebrate *that*?' snorts Debs. 'Have Queen Victoria being *amused*?'

'Yeah,' giggles Imo, 'bags I be Elizabeth when Raleigh turns up with the potato.'

Ricky Vincent's silhouette is addressing the ceiling. His voice is soft, spinning aural candyfloss, wrapping Belle in filmy layers and layers. Whatever he'd said about *using*, once here she finds the atmosphere is sugar-coated. Beside her, Mae's gum-chewing gets louder as she fails to suppress a grin. Ricky Vincent has nearly spun enough.

'Of course, there'll have to be a bit of retro stalking in fishnets and furs as well. But *we* can have fun with a Nell Gwyn bodice, a bit of Boadicea armour' – he retreats – 'even if the theme is just a gimmick.'

His girls become accomplices.

Debs calls out, 'But *you* do gimmicks, like, *tongue-in-cheek*.'

Imo asserts, 'Yeah, your bride one's fab: the girl comes on backwards looking all frothy in her virgin gown, and she turns round and her wedding dress has a massive hole for a front. Great, isn't it?'

Belle and Sylvie, the most evidently new girls, are shoved forwards. Anxiously, they look back.

'Just say "Yes",' Mae hisses.

Ricky Vincent's face is in the light, as distinct for a moment as the Cheshire Cat's, grinning.

'Now,' he says, a dark figure receding once more. 'Warm ups.'

'REACH for the SKY.'

Most touch their toes.

'TOUCH your TOES.'

Most reach for the sky. A couple stretch towards each other so they can continue chatting. If it was Belle in that casually side-stretched position, she'd slip and hit the floor. She kicks her sandals off and hitches up her dress. One of her arms flails past Mae's face.

'Watch it!'

'Sorry,' Belle grunts, folding until her palms are flat on the floorboards. The skirt of her dress tents. Her legs and arms are guy ropes, taut to snapping point.

Head upside down beneath her armpit, Mae advises, 'It is the first day. Be kind to yourself.'

Crookedly upright, Belle clasps her hands behind her back. Her mouth forms a surprised 'O'.

Mae turns her right knee out and pops the foot into its opposite thigh. Balanced easily on one leg, she considers, 'It's only my opinion, but you'll want a long hot bath, with salt, when you get home.'

Red-faced, Belle retorts, 'I'm here to push myself.'

Ricky Vincent rushes to the back to the lighting box and scribbles on a clipboard. He taps a microphone so feedback makes all the girls on stage wince and cover their ears, and he Tannoys to front of house, 'GM to auditorium in fifteen minutes. GM to auditorium in fifteen minutes.'

Debs and Imo roll their eyes. The General Manager will come as a matter of course.

Vaulted on stage, under the most flattering spot, 'George, Gift, Monroe,' instructs Ricky Vincent. 'Just do the production number for starters.'

With upturned palm, Ricky Vincent hands his authority to Cheryl, who steps out of the crowd with a pleased flick of her platinum hair. The other girls shift impatiently. Stroking his delicate fingers, Ricky Vincent calls, 'Rochelle, impro a bit on *Justine in Leather*, and Debs, experiment with *First-Century Queen*.'

Rochelle hums a Prince tune to herself and, over at the entrance, uses a pillar to practise her pole work on. In the aisle, Debs kicks off her biker's boots and does proper warm ups, stretching her ham-strings.

Cheryl's smile is a wide 'U' of understanding. 'You'll be fine,' she tells the new girls. 'It's a basic eight count: eight steps, pause, eight steps, pose, and so on between tape markings one to four.'

Later tonight, the opening number will seem complex, glittering costumes moving in a kaleidoscope of colour until everything is a massive, shimmering illusion. Now, with the house lights up, the auditorium is so badly lit it is possible to see where a section of aisle carpet has been stapled back in place. On stage, the four tape markings corral a very small area.

As she goes through the moves, Cheryl's sneakers issue 40 squeaks – a mere five sets of eight steps in a roughly Union Jack formation.

Cheryl does the whole production number twice within a couple of minutes, then instructs, 'Now join in.'

The way Cheryl does it, it is mindless maths. Belle feels as if she's in an exam on square roots when she'd revised multiplication. The warm ups haven't helped her at all.

Legs cross each other twice, then the arms go out, and turn – but Belle is stage left while the rest are stage right and she's galloping after and they're up and she's down.

'OK,' Cheryl snaps. 'Let's start again.'

Belle's eyes strain sideways as, more slowly, Cheryl crosses her legs and side-steps. Belle's lips count her through as she follows, round, and again, and back, lapsing more and more beats behind. Though she looks as if she's on lead stilts, even Sylvie has it better than Belle. And Mae finds it so straight-forward her gaze is somewhere else completely.

Ricky Vincent calls, 'Mae, you're staying with the other new girls till they've learned it.'

'For Christ's sake! Get your act together or we'll never make it from rehearsal to performance pay. You might not care but I bloody well do. It's RIGHT, two, three, four; LEFT, two, three, four' – and Mae has grabbed Belle by the arm – 'UP and TWIST and' – Mae has let go – 'RIGHT, two, three' – and Belle is doing the routine on her own.

'I can do it!' she says in amazement.

'You can do it,' says Sylvie with relief.

'Once more,' says Cheryl.

And as Belle does the production sequence twice more, a fourth time still more smoothly, she realises that trike falls and slips of knives and can openers were on her own; this is in a group of friends. She smiles at Sylvie, who nods her strained face back, at Mae, who bursts a gum bubble she's just blown.

Belle slips her hands to where her newly streamlined pubic hair is hidden beneath her dress. She scans the windowless, clockless walls. Perhaps she's been here fifteen minutes, maybe hours. In the secrecy of Xanadu's, she thinks, she will be able to streamline everything about herself. Her arms rise into the air as she finishes the sequence successfully again.

'Your best yet,' praises Cheryl.

'A few days and you'll be ready to go live with that,' confirms Ricky Vincent.

'With the production number in a few *days*?' Belle's eyes pop out like celebratory streamers. 'And what about a solo?'

'Couple of weeks,' estimates Ricky Vincent.

'If you spin it out,' murmurs Cheryl.

'Couple of weeks!' says Belle, already envisioning herself emerging fully formed from her cocoon ready to fly beautifully in public.

Ricky Vincent arcs an eyebrow. Belle arcs hers back, thinking that after all *he's* the fool because she's the one who's going to be using him.

Ricky Vincent is involved with Debs in the aisle. A frecklefaced grin fixed over her shoulder, Debs is presenting her leather-trousered arse to him and he is repositioning it higher. He pushes her head lower and, with his polished shoe, eases her bare feet wider. He taps her buttock.

'And that, of course, is that.' He steps back. 'The lights

dim and you are frozen for eternity in the minds of the punters,' he confirms, 'in that finale "V".

'Follow the others,' Ricky Vincent waves airily towards the new girls. 'They'll show you out by the performers' exit.'

But the old girls are already at the back of the stage, in with the props, gone. In a panic at the front, Belle and Sylvie grab their things.

'What's the rush?' snaps Mae, as they dash across the boards, higher – to the furnace that is tonguing paper flames, beyond the plyboard cannon, round behind the deco elevator that's been touched up with tinfoil and, mysteriously, back into the tonguing paper flames again.

'Are you coming then?' snaps Mae.

She seems to be standing in a dip. She steps further and Belle and Sylvie have to drop their heads to see Mae's leggings and waistcoat disappearing down a well-lit corridor. They rush after her, knees in the lead, bags and belongings flying round them, eyes unblinking.

It is a warren backstage. All the steps and corridors lead to rooms that are versions of the others, or possibly the same ones approached by different routes, it's hard to tell. They are bigger or smaller but the garish green and purple swirly carpets are consistent throughout, as is the crowdedness – wigs on shelves, costumes over rails and stools, girls' day clothes scattered on the floor, trampled, biker's outfit, windbreaker, jogging suit, shed like snakeskins.

Each doorway seems to Belle to present a frieze of naked intimacy. She passes them on tiptoes. In one, a girl just showered, with a towel turbanned round her head, invites her mate to dry her back. Belle saddens. She'd got used to them all being clothed, appearing so thoroughly every-day, that they were getting to feel like mates, Debs and Imo and Cheryl and Sue, to her, and now they're nameless, untouchable. In one doorway, a girl in a kimono has her feet up in another's lap while she reads a magazine, so intimate she has her toes wedged in the flesh creases of her colleague's stomach. But now Belle feels annoyed: that girl's stomach has a couple of rolls of chubbiness. Another is moisturising herself with movements that flap her breasts about like flannels, and another is bent forward, hair trailing to the floor between splayed and positively cellulited legs, holding a blow-dryer ready. At the edge of the room in the doorway, Belle twists her head. The perspective is odd. The girl appears to be performing cunnilingus on herself. She turns her face up. Belle stares stupidly. And then the girl is many-headed, multi-breasted, splitting into three.

Debs and Imo stand in front of Sue's compromised position. They bend their legs like policemen, sturdy PC Plods as they pull on their G strings. Yet there is so much static, hairspray, deodorant, mouth-freshener in the air that their expressions are diffused. Their smiles are mermaids', wavery, beguiling.

It is a jolt to Belle to realise that she and Sylvie, stopped beside her, are being handed something.

'Take them,' urges Debs.

'They're spares,' Imo reassures.

'Best to practise,' Debs explains.

'Most of us have at least a bit of allergy or itchiness at first,' Imo elaborates.

Mae nudges Sylvie, who opens her bag. Wigs and packets of eyelashes tumble in. Belle's 'Thank you' goes unheard as doors slam up the corridor on sounds of outrageous, magnifying laughter.

They pass through several doors, all big, some charred where fags get stubbed during breaks, others hooked with mops and brushes. Each door is distinctive from the Xanadu's side yet when Belle looks back they have become an inconsequential recess or a wood-grained wall, disappeared. It seems all exits aren't also entries here. It is possible to sneak out of Xanadu's but not necessarily back in.

Mae pushes Belle and Sylvie blinking into the light of day. Outside, the air burns their skin and their lungs as they breathe. They have to keep close to a drainpipe to miss a sudden rush of pedestrians who whoop carnival-style. A theatre trio in big felt hats and funny masks wanders by on stilts.

Belle looks left – bookshop – and right – patisserie. 'How did we get here? I thought we were going to come out by the *XXX* cinema.' She is, once again, confounded, Sylvie too.

Mae straightens her waistcoat and says, polite but firm, 'See you later. I've got some errands.'

Sylvie's hand is on Belle's. 'I should phone my mum. Will you wait for me?'

Belle falls back against a lamp-post. In the phone booth, Sylvie cradles the receiver, rocking her body as if she is in her mother's arms. A block away, a backwards glance confirms that Mae thinks she's out of sight as she embraces a man, who, as they rotate, kissing deeper, turns out to be a woman.

*

It's rude to stare. Belle switches her head from flesh pushed out of a bikini top, then feverishly from crotch squeezed into a pair of cycling shorts, more feverishly from a café-table-full of tourists who have hitched and rolled already skimpy coverings to stretch to catch the sun, bared limbs prone, ice-cubes held to foreheads melting and licking down their arms.

Belle focuses on a news-stand. It is small, a fold-out box really, the kind of plywood structure a Punch and Judy show might come from. It is on a pavement, very public, approached constantly by a decent cross-section of society, senior, infant. It features nothing controversial. It is just general circulation, mass-distributed glossies behind the strips of wire.

Pedestrians continue passing by, carrying bunches of ice-creams, unfolding maps of London, turning faces from cans of fizzy drinks as they open them, chucking empties beside the overflowing bin that is not far from the news-stand. The vendor's mouth seems to be on wires, snapping.

'EE'NIN' STAN'ARD! EE'NIN' STAN'ARD!'

His hand pistons out to catch coins – flashing in the sun – and back to fill the tin that is stashed away with the women's monthlies, one featuring a woman modelling a jacket, and it's just a fashion spread, but the model is undo-ing her zip, baring her breasts. And Belle is practically tearing her hair because she still can't look.

Indeed, she feels cheated several times over. Naked, the Xanadu girls were not perfect but just as flawed as she is. So now there are the picture-perfect cover girls *and* the dressing-room nudes and *both* lots hurl her into arousal when Belle was supposed to be becoming inured, to be feminising herself.

If she still can't look unequivocally at other women, how, she despairs, can she be happy to be seen herself?

Beside her, Sylvie Gift's bra can be made out through her T-shirt. It is a teenage one patterned with cartoon flowers. Her hair is kirby-gripped with yellow smileys.

Her eyes are still red from her phone call home. 'What now?'

Belle is trying to brush the dust off her dress with her hand. She rubs with a spittled finger. But it is embedded, infinitesimally small particles of Xanadu's, of its stage, props, spray paint, all glueing into the weave of her Lycra, which has lost its snap. It hangs about her breasts and hips.

'I'm due somewhere, actually. Fancy coming?'

'I can't believe it! How do I look? If only I'd known beforehand.' The compact mirror shakes in Sylvie's hand. Lipstick veers towards her ear. Belle gently wipes it off.

'That's the kind of job *I* want. Is she *quite* famous or very? *Cynthia Knight*!'

'*Lilian White*,' Belle snaps.

Sylvie's face is swoony. 'Yes, but TELEVISION!'

Apart from anything else, Sylvie is a good excuse for Belle to phone ahead to check that she got as far as the guest list. Lilian is a busy woman. She doesn't always remember. It's not surprising. It is just a bit humiliating for Belle when it happens.

———

In Lilian White's broadcasting history, the review that affected her most was the one that called her 'matronly tarty'. 'Tarty' she was amused by. 'Matronly' was too awful. Her new chat show is being filmed not in a stuffy old studio at the end of a tube line, but in the pulsing heart of the city, in a trendy nightclub.

The camera angles will be straightforward. Cut-aways will take the viewer from speaker to speaker conversationally with shots of the audience to punctuate. Lilian White will be delivered, neatly, beautifully and above all personally all around the country to viewers in their living rooms.

Of course, the reality of filming is messy, with endless retakes and a running order that is chopped about until the show can be almost incomprehensible to watch. And because the outside world has to be excluded, the double doors are arranged in an insulating air-lock system, and going in is like entering a lunatic asylum. There's howling – microphones' feedback, loud-speakered 'TESTING TESTING' – and a stench that is almost unbearable at first. Simulated daylight spots singe the already sweaty air. The audience – which is not here to be entertained so much as to be a supporting cast – is squashed between cameras and dollies and boxes of equipment and required to appear casual. In groups of threes and fours round tables, members may occasionally sip the tee-total cocktails provided.

Belle scrambles ahead, over the assault course of wires and cables. She daren't notice what is happening either on stage – bits of set being repaired last minute – or up in the control box – the director tearing his hair out because a guest is late.

Again and again as a child, she witnessed the enormity of making television programmes – big budgets, innumerable staff, giant sets – with everything, the show's success or failure, depending on Lilian White. She could misread the Autocue, she could forget a guest's name, she could become suddenly speechless. And each time something awful doesn't happen, Belle feels worse. Instead of easing with experience, her panic grows more debilitating. Lilian hasn't fluffed before, not in Belle's memory, but there is always a first.

Sylvie crashes nearer, dropping her bag, knocking a light stand. Belle is glad to be able to be nonchalant, if briefly – 'It's only TV' – and gracious. Positioning an empty seat for Sylvie to fall into, she smoothes Sylvie's hair and settles her hands.

The curtains are pulled back to reveal a piece of heaven. While the three guests fiddle with their tie-pin mikes and gen up on notes and demand glasses of water, stage left, sheathed in midnight blue satin, Lilian is still. It is not necessary for her to be geographically in the middle to be the centre of attention. Her smile is beatific.

There is thunderous mayhem, the lightning crack of a clapperboard, then silence. The world awaits Lilian White.

Belle goes spinning in an overhead mirror ball.

A problem watching her mother perform has always been that scenes from their domestic life keep interfering, superimposing themselves in conflict with the Lilian who is on stage, so cool, so definite. And Belle knows which one must be real.

She is distant. Her voice is soft, yet it fills the space as if she is indeed a deity.

'Welcome.'

But the saboteur in Belle's head keeps going – and she's seeing Lilian at the sink rubber-gloved, rigid; at the dinner table in tears of rage because Belle misaligned the salt and pepper pot – flashing bigger and bigger till it seems everyone else must be able to see as well when condition of entry is supposed to be adoration. In fake candlelight faces waver, bodies dissolve until all that is left is their function as receptors of Lilian White, reproduced in eyes infinitely around the room. But Belle can't help it.

Whole sections of their past re-run sometimes. She is in the doorway, her mother doing sexy dancing in the middle of the living area. And it looks exciting, the way she's unbuttoning her blouse above gyrating hips, eyes half closed, head thrown back. But Belle can't join in the celebration of another love affair begun because she knows that soon it will be ended, *kaput*, *finito*: weeping, Lilian wailing, 'I thought he was *the one*!'

The elusive *one* can at least make Belle angry – where is he and why doesn't he come to save her mother? Her terror that she may never be enough is squeezed out, at least for a while, by the business of keeping close to Lilian, passing tissues, caressing, whispering love into every inch of her while she can because next she will be in the hall, knees clasped.

Sometimes the wildest fantasy did enter her head: wouldn't it have been wonderful if the man whose seed she'd come from also turned out to be Lilian's everlasting love – and the thought flew on and disappeared, leaving young Belle crouched out in the hall, knuckles white against her head, hearing silence in her mother's room.

Lilian always stayed bright enough for work. She had to. Single parent, must continue bringing in a wage.

But back in the apartment she was someone else, curled in the furthest corner of the bedroom, face to the wall, dishevelled hair, crumpled robe, blind to everything but her own misery. If she could only have been Lilian and looked at herself she'd have been appalled, disgusted. But she was a stranger. Belle couldn't reach her. And she was never allowed to confide in anyone else who might have been able to either, not Lilian's parents, not Geoffrey. All this was between the two of them. Afterwards Lilian always made Belle promise that her 'little lapses' would remain *their secret*, which made Belle proud and desperate.

'Isn't she wonderful,' Sylvie breathes, prevented from floating to the stage only by the table.

Belle has had this all her life, and of course she feels exulted, but while the words *Isn't she talented! Isn't she beautiful!* are being said to her, the admirer's gaze on Lilian is hypnotised. Any response would break the spell and so Belle, instead of being in conversation, is an intruder.

Head bowed, she counts silently to ten. That is usually enough.

'And what does *your* mum do?'

'Hairdresser.'

Belle's face is craned in front of Sylvie's. 'That's nice for you then, free cut and colours whenever you want. Has she got her own salon?'

Sylvie shifts until she has Lilian reflected in her eyes again. Her lips peel from her teeth. '*Shhh!*'

Under the table, Belle's hand creeps towards where her friend's T-shirt is loose over the waist of her ski-pants. She grasps a bit of Sylvie's fabric as if it is something of herself.

But now the saboteur in her head is staying with one clip, reeling through it more slowly, repeating this scene from the past: Belle's thumb hovering near her mouth, Lilian not even noticing, returned home in a state of physical agitation Belle had never seen before, a lioness in a pit, lashing from an enlarged publicity shot of herself which had been taken some years earlier, taut-faced, to another that was later, softer focus, to a mirror, dragging the skin beneath her eyes.

Behind her, Belle tried, 'You look lovely.'

'My agent,' Lilian began breezily, 'has just forwarded . . .'

Belle grips the table. *This* is the Lilian to believe in, the chat-show hostess sheathed in midnight blue satin, the one who is so utterly convincing as a woman of outstanding strength. She is complete, up there in the spotlight performing TV tricks: smile for 1.2 seconds, turn to first guest, execute two witticisms and one suggestion of body contact to instigate a relaxed dinner party atmosphere, and so on, expertly, to order, smooth, luxurious.

It wouldn't take much to transpose her body language onto a chrome pole. Belle drains the fruit juice provided by the network. She'd be allowed a real drink if she was in the audience at Xanadu's. She cuffs herself about the ear. She stares till mascara pricks her eyelids to keep herself firmly in the set for Lilian White's TV show.

'My agent has just forwarded a request from *Penthouse* magazine.'

Belle was only ten. '*Penthouse*,' she hazarded. 'That's great news.'

'Of course, I couldn't possibly do it. But the fact remains,' – Lilian flushed with excitement – '*Penthouse* wants me, topless,' blocking a photo of her daughter, 'ME.'

Belle grabs for Sylvie's hand. Sylvie squeezes back, amazed and privileged to be here to share Belle's joy.

It is the break for the pre-recorded drop-in. On stage in her royal blue armchair, Lilian does quick face relaxation exercises, waggling her jaw so she can smile naturally when the cameras are rolling again. Below her, a member of staff secures his headphones crossly. Using his clipboard as a conductor's baton, he has to raise audience applause three times before it is loud enough.

Making up for her neighbours' lassitude, Belle's eyes and mouth are wide. Her body is stiff, her fingers flat and neat together as she claps faster, a clockwork toy wound too tight.

'IT'S IN THE CAN.'

The relief is palpable. The studio reverts to being an esoteric discothèque. T-shirted staff push headphones back and slap high-fives, hooting and hollering. The audience chatters excitedly, one to the other, grabbing bags and coats, in a dance of departure. Although, most throw a longing look over their shoulder at Lilian White, a slither of midnight blue satin, whose retreat invites pursuit when she is far behind the barrage of set and equipment that prevents it.

One thing Belle has over most of the other punters is that she can go backstage. Her access to Lilian White gives people a concrete reason for wanting her, then Belle can't help doubting whether they wanted her for herself in the first place.

'Sylvie,' she instructs. 'Follow me.'

Sylvie does instantly. Belle trips and stumbles.

The Green Room – a place intended for relaxation and hospitality – is here a concrete cell lit by a bare bulb. Back at the studio, things would be plusher. This emptied stock-room is all the nightclub had to offer.

There is a publicity shot of Lilian on the wall, and on a table nearby some flowers, modest bunches. The director, Oliver Bradwell, had told the PA that two were plenty – Lilian is the media equivalent of a minor royal, not the Queen Mother.

Because Oliver does like to joke around, he has found that it can be a job in itself getting people to take him seriously. He is obeyed but not always respected.

The ceiling is low. He arranges his body at angles that won't give glimpses of his denim jacket's playful tartan lining. The PA stops in front of him with a tray of wine-filled glasses and bowls of twiglets. He turns his nose up and waves them on to Lilian.

His budget could have stretched to canapés with decorative garnish. She says with chilly politesse, 'No, thank you,' and returns to a journalist, who is heaping on the praise. Lilian can bear it.

'Sweet of you,' she says with a smile that displays her naturally perfect teeth and plumps her cheeks prettily without diminishing her eyes or causing too many wrinkles. Lilian controls her pleasure in order that it can be savoured.

In the doorway, Belle's smile seems separate from her face. It is goofily all over the place, her eyes too. Her feet have slipped apart across the floor. Stopped by the door jamb on one side, Sylvie on the other, she is wedged safely.

In the middle of the room, her mother is hardly visible for acolytes. It seems it is not the bulb that is the light but Lilian herself, moths fluttering around her.

Just as she did on stage, she bestows her attention fairly, showing her smile 1.2 seconds to the left, the right, and back, and forth. She sees Belle. She appears to be reaching out for the moon and the stars. She calls, 'Darling!'

Fans part. Belle lumbers into a length of space that is more significant than a red carpet.

She is nearly a head taller than Lilian when she stands straight. Somehow she has to strain to reach up to kiss her mother's cheek.

'You were fantastic, Lilian, wonderful, marvellous,' edging nearer, breathing her in.

Over by the doorway Sylvie's brown eyes are unblinking, her body already in the suggestion of a curtsy, a smile fighting for the opportunity to break out.

'Oh, yes.' Belle says, 'Lilian, there's someone I want you to meet.'

'In a moment, darling.'

Lilian's arm around Belle's shoulders ensures a precise amount of air between them. Belle's brow cuts itself up. She splays her hands apologetically towards Sylvie but can't help curling the ends of her fingers tight in excitement. Lilian is still on duty. Her head turns, doing work chat. Her voice is syrup, trickling over Belle's bare shoulders. Then it's not. The director is approaching.

'Just a couple of things before I leave,' he says airily.

Lilian can take criticism, in memo form, bin-sized.

She thrusts Belle forward. 'Oliver, I'd like you to meet my daughter.'

Belle knows Lilian intimately. She has soaked up her tears. She is being offered like a star's handkerchief. She's glad to be of service.

Oliver doesn't shake Belle's hand so much as turn it over in his. It is soft. He looks up. Lilian's eyes are glassy.

'A gang of us are going to a sushi bar. Want to join us, Lil?'

The informality of 'Lil' makes her flinch. But work is work and networking is essential. 'That would be delightful.'

Hot-faced, Belle rushes towards Sylvie. Her feet get left a little behind then twist and her arms flap as if trying to soar from her own clumsiness, and everywhere heads are turning, including Lilian's, and hands are spreading, except Lilian's, which clasp her drink more tightly.

Sylvie is there for Belle. Arms outstretched, it seems she had an idea about why she was invited all along. Belle pulls

Sylvie close, pear- into plank-shape, dusky blonde into fair-skinned brunette, physical negatives beginning to merge, except, while Sylvie's startled expression is at Belle, Belle's is on Lilian.

Lilian turns her back.

'You go and grab your mum to yourself a bit.' Sylvie nods urgently. 'Go on.'

One-to-one dates get shifted as easily as Post-it notes. Adulation is ebbing away. This is Belle's best chance. Squeezing Sylvie's hand gratefully, she follows as Lilian leaves quickly for the privacy of the upstairs office that's serving as her dressing room.

The hinged metal arm pulls the door to. The room is silent, the portrait stillness of Lilian's face ruined for a moment by the sight of her adult daughter as if for the first time – dishevelled against a filing cabinet, crumpled dress, thug's sandals, bad make-up, aggressively hacked short fringe above split ends at shoulder length that points to underarm hair sticking out in thick black waves.

'You certainly do have your own style.' Lilian's hand flickers across and her eyes are immaculate again, fixed on Belle's armpits. 'You know,' manoeuvering a long hooked pole, 'it's not a question of vanity but of hygiene,' opening a ceiling-high window wider.

Belle blushes furiously as she stuffs straggles of her hair out of sight.

'Of course *I* don't mind,' says Lilian. Her fingers pressing her chest back thrust her sincere expression nearer. 'But if a mother can't point out these things, who can?'

'Sure.' Belle flounders.

Lilian sits at the mirror. 'You used to look so lovely, that cherubic little face, your hair in ribbons,' she chats away to a part of the room that doesn't exist, 'that Liberty frock I bought you when you were seven, you were adorable in that, do you remember?'

If Belle wasn't tripping over the hem she was catching the bow in the door. She looks down now at her sandals, which are huge, their cork soles curling up round her feet like boats in which she can sail away.

'Thanks for getting us tickets. I'm sorry I didn't have a chance to introduce you to Sylvie but . . .'

'I saw. Peroxide blonde, fake tan.'

'You must be exhausted' – Belle's hands in the air frantically cut slack – 'you've had a long day. And it's so hot. Let me get you a drink.' Her thumb bends backwards as she pours water into a glass that Lilian refuses.

'Sylvie wants a job in the media.'

'Lots do.'

'I guess like yours. I thought perhaps . . .'

'Christ! Everyone and their uncle expects me to pull strings for them.'

'I didn't mean . . .'

'I shouldn't have to tell you of all people that I didn't just walk into this job.'

With a mascara brush, Lilian pulls at her lashes.

Belle stares at her clasped fingers, as if not knowing how to ever start trying to untangle them. 'Sylvie's not just any old friend. She's my new best friend.'

'You've had so many.'

'She lives with me.'

A new pile of fan mail lies at Lilian's elbow. Friendships can't offer anything solid, she thinks, goading a nail with an orange stick. 'How's work?'

'Work?'

Lilian looks up crossly. 'Yes. Edenfine.'

'As a matter of fact, I've been having a bit of a time of it recently . . .'

Lilian's face is fragile. 'But you're all right, aren't you. Sweetheart?'

Belle looks as if she was about to try to climb a mountain when the whole thing turned and she's just lost her grip at the top of a ravine.

Lilian grasps her briefly – 'Darling, you're so *strong*' – and she turns away to tend to the last details of her reflection.

If she has guessed the sushi bar Oliver's thinking of, it is awfully brightly lit. 'Really,' she rounds up as she finishes with the eyebrow pencil, 'I don't know how you manage. In my day a job was for life and yet you flit about and even get "let go" and you just bounce right back.'

'Redundancy's something that happens to you, not who you are.'

'Of *course*,' says Lilian. 'You'll just have to do extra well at your new place, won't you?' She checks her watch. She's gone past fashionably and will if she's not careful be rudely late for her director.

'Run along and have fun with your friend Sylvie, darling. Don't mind me. Really.'

*

When Belle has gone, Lilian shuts the cosmetics case. Shaking slightly, she takes a jacket from the rail and buttons herself in.

She will call Geoffrey. He always gives good advice, or takes the burden completely by finding out what is troubling her daughter himself.

Outside, Belle feels strangely free. Withholding information from Lilian is nothing new, but usually they are pieces that eat away at Belle – like overhearing the producer say Lilian is overrated, or a spurned lover at a party commenting on Lilian's *froideur*. Xanadu's is like having a box of chocolates to herself that is big enough to block out the sun. With Sylvie's hand to hold as well, it is remarkably easy for Belle to walk away.

Except, Sylvie will keep going on, through the journey home, every second, chattering excitedly. Now she is keen to meet the whole family.

'What about *Mr* White?'

In the flat, Sylvie backs Belle against the hall wall with suggestions – tea? hot chocolate? Horlicks? – until Belle is so far into the plaster that a swathe of hair pushes forwards.

'How about a late movie?' Sylvie suggests. 'Or a nightcap?'

'Aren't you ready to hit the sack?'

The spare room is a boxroom really, piled high with junk, its window scrappy with the remains of a nylon curtain.

Sylvie has seen and she has come back anyway. Opening

the hall cupboard, 'Blankets, sheets, towels,' Belle points randomly about its shelves. 'You know where the kitchen is and the bathroom,' her hand flicking it all away. 'Use whatever you want.'

Her face warms momentarily. An alternative was a bender ending up on a one-night stand somewhere, wide awake, strangers facing opposite walls, hands in praying position beneath their cheeks. This way she gets the reassurance of another human presence and her bed to herself. Their forearms slip close. Tiny hairs enliven each other's skin.

'Sleep well.'

At school, the word 'desertion' went round ahead of Belle and she became expert at encouraging speculation whilst preventing direct questions by reeling slightly and raising out-turned fingers to her forehead. The therapist, of course, homed straight in on the forbidden subject.

Belle knew it must have been kindness on Lilian's part, and that's why she went. She was old enough to see what he was up to. He infected only two three-quarter hours of her life but she remembers almost every second. She felt he emanated arrogance, his position – head bowed towards hands clasped in his lap – making it clear to her that he had answers and was going to keep them to himself.

It was a small attic room. There was his chair, with him in it, and there was a couch. She honoured her part of the deal. She lay down and garbled on.

'Perhaps I represent your father.'

Belle sat stiff. 'Don't be daft. I don't know him.'

'You show anger towards me.'

She faced the wall. 'OK, so let's say you might be right and I could have been suppressing my true feelings in case they put him off from coming back . . .'

It was as if he had opened floodgates. Belle's outpouring used up almost a whole box of tissues.

'. . . anyway, how can I feel angry, who with? He was one of three flings. Lilian didn't even know their full names. And I only found out that much from Geoffrey, because I can't ask Lilian directly because she can hardly bear it, and anyway I don't *want* to because there's no point because there's no way of tracking him down – which in any case would be a betrayal – and it's so mad that it upsets me that he has no idea that I exist that it's best to simply put it out of my head because it's much more to the point that Lilian and I got on perfectly all right without him.'

Then the therapist suggested that perhaps she also felt resentment towards her mother. Belle was off the couch before he'd finished the sentence.

Back at home she told her, 'Thank you Lilian. I feel much better. I don't need any more.'

It was as if she had released the sun into her mother's face. Belle was, naturally, glad to have been able to give, and so easily.

That was when she started confiding more in her action men. Sometimes she had to walky-talky them her news because they were so busy saving the world. But ultimately she always had the power to bring them back. She could dress them up anyway she pleased, with professorial fuse-wire glasses or matchstick machine-guns, depending what kind of advice she felt she needed.

Now, by the wardrobe, she opens the Jiffy bag and takes out a male plastic doll. His biceps are pumped. His expression is stern.

She twists his head back to front. She flicks his non-existent balls.

Belle's bedroom is as hotch-potch as the rest of her flat, except with a more distinct smell of disintegration. In a corner, black mould creeps through, unsettling the plaster.

The Bakelite lamp was here when she arrived. The metallic cushions were Lilian's cast-offs, the ethnic rug a gift from Geoffrey.

She's more achey now, muscles twingeing up her legs and back, but looking down Belle sees, squeezed into Lycra, the same sagging, bulging, pigeon-toed form. Her image in the silver of Lilian's cushions is so abstracted by seams and creases she's indistinguishable. But then, thinks Belle, she often fails to recognise herself when she's walking past reflective shop windows.

Her full-length mirror is propped against the wall at an angle that fills it mainly with the ceiling. Shoving it straight, she is incarcerated in its dust. She rips her dress over her head and wipes. Her reflection is streaky but much clearer than it has been.

She goes on tiptoes, teetering. Her feet, which she had always thought too wide, could have been designed for wearing stilettos. Their toes are long and supple, stretching like individual little people to support her. And she finds the knock-on effect pleasing. The way her limbs have to twist to adjust, her hips, her shoulders – all the bits of her that were too square on – are softened. The kink in her spine will be less significant than a weak stitch in the context of a Xanadu's costume.

Double-chinned, she thrusts her groin, eyebrows trying to take her eyes out horizontally for a better view, but then she is suddenly flipping her legs about as if she needs to pee, hands over her crotch area, which is red and bobbled as a plucked chicken. Shaving was too savage.

She lifts an arm and twists a pinch of hair. This time she'll use a cream hair-remover and dissolve the parts of her she doesn't want with the feminine hygiene equivalent of weed-killer.

She throws back her head and raises a knee as if she is a prancing pony. Perhaps she can be her own porn-shot turn-on – that, she thinks, would be a bonus measure of independence. She can always balance it out by doing something brainy later, and Xanadu's will be perfect for that too, her work at night leaving her free to do applications and interviews for more 'proper' jobs during the day.

She curls her tongue, licking her lips lasciviously.

chapter 3

Sylvie is an early riser. She likes to start her mornings with a cup of tea in bed, milky, one sugar, a chocolate biscuit resting in the saucer. The best Belle's kitchen cupboards have to offer in the way of something dunkable is an oatcake.

Sylvie hadn't anticipated feeling more alone in a shared flat than in the hostel. The lino sticks to her slippers, rippling behind her as she paces. The windows are so dirty she can't even see if it is a nice day.

She does her pink house-coat up to the neck. She begins to perspire, then plainly sweat.

Although Belle's flat is small, even poky, it can feel vast, the kitchen going off long and thin to the right of the front door, the hall actually straight ahead but because of the way it opens out seeming to veer left into a bathroom that is a corridor opposite the second bedroom, which manages to cut back towards the block's communal stairwell.

Belle's bedroom is at the far end of the building. It has a precipitous air to it. She tends to keep the curtains closed. After dark their pattern is a bloom of chintzy cabbage roses. But daylight bleaches them, forcing the black slats of the window-frame through instead. The grid insinuates its way into every gap in the weave of the carpet, every stain of the duvet cover, which her sleep has wrapped around her, a grubby loincloth. Her forearm pushes her breasts into her armpits and her head is twisted over the edge of the mattress, eyes slashes of white under slightly opened lids, throat jutting as if she has choked on a bite of apple.

From far away, noises of tins and pots of cleaning fluids being taken out of a kitchen cupboard magnify up the hall. Belle's stare is drier than the pillow case that now fills her mouth.

Changed into the most Glo-white items she could find in her suitcase, Sylvie has already done a shop run. She can afford to stand Belle a few basics – Loo Blue, Plug-Fresh, Viakill.

Water froths in a bowl on one side. The J-cloth is a swish of lemon yellow as Sylvie shifts the folded towel that is a cushion for her knees, working her way backwards over the kitchen floor.

She spreads sheets of newspaper as if they are huge, flat seeds. If the place was spic and span, Sylvie would still be giving it a once over. It is a way of polishing home-sickness out and stability in on the surfaces.

Belle has been an unnerving presence, towel still settling on the bathroom rail, bedroom door closing moments before

Sylvie could catch her in the hall to ask permission. She has made plenty of noise. Belle could have come out at any time to stop her.

Knocking crockery, she wedges her feet at the back of the draining board in a splitting rock-climber's stretch at the window. She hadn't realised how by-the-by the help she'd given her mother as a child had been, cleaning out the budgerigar's cage, ironing a duvet cover. She wipes a strand of hair from her forehead with a bent wrist. She is exhausted, sweat leeching the colour from her.

One rubber glove inside as a sucker on the glass, with the other she sweeps the wet sponge as far as she can reach through the dirt outside, until through the window sun falls scalloped across the kitchen.

While a raised eyebrow suggests she's still taking stock of the situation, Belle is already on the toilet, dressing gown flipped out of the way, elbows planted on her knees, hands spread under her chin like leaves beneath a flower.

She and Sylvie have through dark hours breathed the same air. They have inhaled each other. For once, Belle feels sure that an intimacy barrier has been crossed.

For Sylvie it's more simple. If someone does her a kindness, they are a friend. She said she needed to save money. Belle carried on beating herself down till the rent was lower than anything Sylvie had seen in *Loot*.

Gown flying, Belle's bare feet quake the hall boards ahead of her. Sylvie sits quickly at the table, pony-tail swinging, face expectant.

She has been meticulous. She has thrown nothing away

except the milk, which was so off she couldn't pour it down the sink but had to mash it through the plughole with a teaspoon. The worst of the rest of the perishables – a curdled slip of butter, a stale end of wholemeal loaf, a jar featuring just a tarry smear of additive-free spread – she has arranged in a freezer bag on the table.

That's Belle's breakfast sealed like police evidence. In the hallway, she is up against the wall, eyes strained sideways.

With the red and white stripes of the lino distinct, her kitchen is transformed. It is the inside of a seaside stick of rock. The table top has a sugary sparkle. A bottle of Coke and a Battenburg stand on it in cheery judgement. Belle ought to feel a surge of gratitude. She stares into the neck of her gown as if expecting to see something awful seething out.

Sylvie leans forward. '*There* you are,' she scolds gently. Even Sylvie's voice is beautiful, its suppressed Manchester accent sending vowels rolling over consonants, softening. 'Did you sleep well?'

Belle shakes her head as she picks up the Battenburg, a slab of marzipan comfort. What on earth, she wonders, was she thinking? Instead of paring herself down according to plan – giving Xanadu's nothing to go on other than the minimum she should choose to present about herself – she took Sylvie first to see her mother and then back home to rifle through Belle's drawers and cupboards.

'Listen.'

Sylvie has been waiting for some gratitude for all her cleaning.

Belle presses the Battenburg's Cellophane over her eyes. 'About last night . . .'

'Oh *that*. Don't you worry,' Sylvie reassures, 'I won't tell a soul at Xanadu's you've got a famous mum.'

Belle drops the cake. 'Tell who you want.'

'And,' says Sylvie confidentially, 'thanks for trying to introduce me.'

'Lilian can't help you.'

'I'm not *totally* naive. If I thought it was that easy I wouldn't be at a place I thought I never would, working my arse off for an Equity card.'

'You won't really get one at Xanadu's.'

'Will too!'

'Ricky Vincent was just saying that.'

'I asked the others. Two last month alone.'

Belle sits opposite. 'Really?'

Sylvie gives her pony-tail a sharp, divergent tug, putting it high and bouncy on her head. 'I've done my research. And anyway, your mum can't be so great if she lets you live in this place.'

'It's fine!'

'She must have *pots* of cash.' Sylvie's hands splay to cobwebs she couldn't reach. 'She could probably just buy you a whole new flat.'

Eyes rolling, hand crashing to the table, Belle insists, 'I'm independent!'

Sylvie's voice is rising. 'What's so good about being independent if it means living like this?'

'*It's bohemian.*'

They are face to face over the table between sticky Coke and mouldy health food, air shared, total strangers.

'Anyway, if it's so awful what are you doing living in it too?'

Sylvie's suddenly appalled. 'Absolutely, horses for courses. All I meant was, aren't you lucky?' She raises the bottle. 'Coke?'

'Thanks.'

Belle hates just the thought of things like this, with enough sugar to rot her from the inside out. Except she takes a draught and it feels after all like she didn't have any insides for it to even touch. Dark sweetness fizzes directly to the ends of her toes, her fingers. Belle's brows waver. It was all very well perfecting a posture in front of the mirror last night – and she got it feeling rigid – but any façade if it is to stay in place must have its filling in good order.

'Cake?' asks Sylvie.

A piece of fondant pink and yellow dissolves in Belle's mouth. 'What now?'

Sylvie sees the clock and gets to her feet.

Belle clasps an empty chair. Her eyes panic. 'Where are you going?'

'It might even be live with the production number in a couple of days so we'd better get a move on practising with the outfits.' Sylvie's voice is drifting down the hall.

They are on the threshold of Belle's living room.

Belle feels she is hovering for an eternity, staring at the way the moulding round the doorway cuts in and in, a staggered tunnel where dust has been gathering and filling the ridges with thick, grey ropes that moult a line across the boards, piling up in the base of the door jamb where sections were cut away for a carpet that the previous tenants took with them.

Belle had always thought that the 1930s' fireplace distinctly resembled a skull, ivory tiles around a gaping flue, its disused gas jets jutting teeth. Sylvie opens the curtains and the fireplace is merely quaint, a small, redundant feature over at the far side of the room. The minty sofa is far more prominent.

The view through the window is the same as it was when Belle first moved in – of other run-down weedy blocks, many of the panes smashed and backed with cardboard. But now what dominates the picture is clear blue sky. The radio is tuned to Capital Gold, lavishing a new cheerful chat-and-musak wallpaper round the room

Belle had anticipated Sylvie bringing out a stash of girlie magazines, she'd imagined giggling gossip, the pair of them lying on their tummies kicking their legs in the air, maybe even watching entirely pointless morning TV, cartoons and pop promos, in a state of thoughtless innocence.

Instead, she and Sylvie sit side by side on the sprung rectangle of sofa. The wigs lie in front of them on the carpet.

Belle struggles to remember. 'We have to practise because . . .'

'Possibilities of allergies, slippage, or both.'

Belle lifts a set of long blonde locks into her lap. They are static nylon. Still, the action of stroking it back in shape is close to luxurious. She holds the wig up, high, on her fist. The internal netting is in a very feminine floral pattern. She pushes her head forwards, into it.

'You look like a cat's landed on you,' Sylvie laughs softly. 'Here.' She kneels at Belle's feet. 'Let me help.'

Her gaze tangles into Belle's new hairline. As her fingers

tug, the balls of her hands warm Belle's neck. Her breath is sweet. It doesn't feel natural to Belle for two people to get this close unless they are about to kiss. She averts her eyes. Sylvie applies the finishing twists to the nylon locks and leans back, squinting one eye.

'Mmmmm,' Sylvie nods, tentatively at first, then absolutely. 'There.'

She sits quickly. 'Now you do me.'

Reflected in the mirror above the fireplace, the wigs take all the attention. Their curls suggest movement yet remain still, forming bouffant crash helmets.

In unison, they step forwards to do the false eyelashes. In their boxes, laid low, the lashes seem to have expired on the plastic moulding. Perched on Belle and Sylvie's fingertips, they come alive. They are the size of large caterpillars.

The lashes are the kind drag artists use. They're not about enhancing. They are for creating an entirely new set of features.

Belle and Sylvie raise the blackly fanning lashes. Their facial stretching doesn't stop their lids quivering. The glue sticks immediately, drawing their eyes so much higher that their brows disappear. They turn to face each other, pictures of surprise.

It doesn't take long to get used to the wigs, which they find itchy at the front mainly, across the forehead, and apart from that just hot. Belle loosens her dressing gown. Sylvie kicks off her slippers and untucks her T-shirt from her ski-pants. But because blinking brings blackness thundering down, Belle and Sylvie keep their eyes wide open until they can't help themselves any more and they're blinking so fast they're reeling back against the sofa, hands gripped to the edges.

Belle suddenly flings her wig away. She grasps a false eyelash and pulls. Her lids come too, as if fake has merged with real, her face stretching so far it seems it will come off.

Sylvie warns, 'Careful!'

Wigless, lash-less, Belle is insignificant. Sylvie looks away politely.

———

Belle takes a copy of the *Standard* and a red felt-tip pen with her to the lido so she can at least start browsing the jobs pages afterwards while she lies drying in the sun.

In the strip of concrete dressing rooms, her nakedness is a faint purple body suit except for the line of flesh around her wrist that is actually her plastic watchstrap. She fingers it apprehensively, and leaves it on. A bit of water won't kill it, probably, she decides.

But despite the electronic tick-tock that, melded into her, should keep her moving on, in her plain black costume, at the pool side, her arms stay at her sides. Her toes keep gripped to the edge.

It is mid-week, so there are no children splashing, no loud groups of friends, just the odd individual ploughing up and down. Belle thinks of her history of belly-flops and gurgling failures to front-crawl a whole width. She thinks of dancing the production number and springs fingertips first into the air, arcing down to cause barely a ripple as her body is charged with cold that sends her shooting straight as an arrow into an economical crawl, her arms pulling vast weights behind her to be kicked away by her feet as her mouth switches easily between water and air along the entire length of the pool. She pushes off the tiles into an underwater dive to the bottom where she back-strokes along. Bubbles from her smile rise through liquid curls of sunlight. A woman swims across. Her figure is refracted flaccid white. She's obscene to Belle, pubes fronding and not a speck of make-up.

Belle splutters to the surface. She didn't think it was possible to sweat in cold water, certainly not to feel the process, but her denuded armpits seem to be flooding her into the pool.

One elbow hooked over the edge levering her up, she's flicked the watch down her wrist, cast an eye over the face and slipped the watch back up with a movement so automatic that she didn't see the time and has to look again. There's plenty. But where the watch has been pressed over her wrist's scars, it has left the grit-flecked skin shiny red, apparently raw. She can't get out of the lido fast enough.

Today, Ricky Vincent is flamboyant in an orchid-print shirt. He had Belle arrive at 2.30 pm, knowing he couldn't leave Xanadu's till the cashier clocked on at 2.45. She is standing by a poster in the foyer in a dress the shape and colour of a sack, her underarms thick with deodorant. Her costume fitting is at 3 pm. At 3.10, Ricky is still behind the cash desk, delegating. The hinged section of counter has been raised.

'And another thing,' he remembers.

Ricky Vincent could have just given her the address and told her to find her own way. He likes the personal touch. He leads, fast. Belle is as lost in the streets of London as if they're part of Xanadu's, twisting through passages, under an arch, out of an alley, sharp left, up several flights of stairs.

They step into an attic room. The quiet is religious. The light through the open window is stained red and green by potted geraniums. It falls past a table altar. Inside, there are tailor's dummies, grey torsos on sticks that are split in sections so they can be cranked wider or longer for fittings. An elaborate bejewelled robe flows from one The costumier is on her knees before it, bowed, tacking the hem, pins spreading out where her mouth should be.

Ricky lifts a finger to his lips. Belle steps back. On either side of the doorway, they wait discreetly, hands folded.

The costumier, Doreen, is 62. She has been outfitting the Xanadu girls for three decades. She is legendary. She has finished tacking, but doesn't acknowledge them yet. Swift from practice, rhythmically grabbing and stabbing, she fills a pin-cushion which she then raises. An orb bristling light, it is a star in her hand. It keeps Belle and Ricky's attention while the rest of her rises arthritically.

At first glance, she is a homely figure. She is wearing comfy trainers with easy Velcro fastenings, a warm polyester dress and an apron with a strip of pockets to keep her cotton reels and thimble and so on in order. Her hair is soft grey. But her face looks as if it has a wicked sense of humour.

She keeps her half glasses at the end of her nose. Because she never faffed about cutting thread with scissors but always used her teeth, she has worn away a nick into a gap, giving dark space to her smile. She flashes it now.

Ricky says Belle's name. Doreen won't use it. They come and they go.

'Here to be measured, are you, girlie?'

Nothing can undermine the sense of luxury. Belle has never before had a costume fitted specifically for her. It will be a unique garment, an elevating experience.

'Lift your arms.'

Blessed with a new appreciation of her own body, Belle is keen. 'I'll take off my dress, then?'

'Nope.'

Doreen encircles her as she feeds the tape measure past her shoulder blades then grasps it between thumb and forefinger. The plastic cuts into Belle's breasts. Doreen stretches to her side table and scribbles with a stubby pencil the vital statistic on her pad.

The experience is over before Belle's had a chance to make anything of it. Bust, waist, hips. Doreen doesn't waste a second. Belle's crotch is grabbed and the tape measure yanked taut to the floor so quickly that her blush for the inside leg measurement happens after the fact.

Ricky is busy scribbling admin notes in his own pad, so he's not looking.

'Right, then,' says Doreen, cueing their exit.

'Excellent,' says Ricky Vincent. 'Let's go.'

When the door has shut behind them, Doreen goes to the cupboard and takes a costume from the middle shelf. This is an easy one, just a production number. A nip here and a tuck there is all it will take. Ricky's girls are all pretty much the same size.

———

As Belle opens the auditorium doors, low-level music pulses through her with the suggestion of a party.

Except, Mae and Sylvie aren't here yet. She doesn't know where to put herself.

Up by the fiery furnace, 'Stop fidgeting or I'll never be able to plait it in,' says Cheryl at one end of Rochelle's hair extension while at the other Rochelle eats a custard dough-nut, quite far away. Down on the apron of the stage, Debs and Imo look more matey, bike helmet and Walkman set aside as they're leaned close in conversation. Belle sidles up to them.

'Hi!'

They don't reply, but nor do they stop talking as she sits beside them.

'I could paper my bloody walls with rejection letters.'

'You'll get there, Debs, don't worry,' says Imo.

Belle is amazed. Crouched over by the festoon, Sue doesn't lower her voice either, insisting down the mobile phone, 'I *know* he's only two, but I'm telling you he understands. Just say Mummy has to work but won't be long.'

In a recess at the back, Ricky Vincent pulls a curl and lets it bounce free. At the front, Sylvie arrives flustered. And finally Mae strolls in.

Ricky is wearing an elevating pair of cowboy boots. His voice trumpets down the aisle.

'Tomorrow I want you all here *bang on*, I do not run a charity and I'll have no more slacking.'

'*Oooo*, someone got out of bed the wrong side this morning,' Debs murmurs.

'And that means silence while I'm talking.'

'Touchy!' risks Belle.

Ricky's eyes are dark circles of experience. 'Cheryl. Centre-stage. Solo.'

The rest await instructions.

'Just watch,' says Ricky Vincent, smirking, and waves them towards the audience's area. 'Go on, girls. Relax.'

Belle doesn't need any encouragement. She's tickled to be draped over several velveteen seats at once, grinning. Next to her, spaced out along the row, everyone else stares at Cheryl on stage alone.

The ceiling's low. She flicks back her platinum hair and puts her hands on her pink jogging-panted hips with a show of bravado.

'OK.'

Ricky Vincent announces, '*Gipsy Rose*!'

'You could at least let me *try* an *Anaïs* impro.'

'What's the big deal with Anaïs? So you've read around a bit. I'd expect nothing less from one of my girls. However,' he flaps his instructions to one side. 'If that's what you want.' He turns away, his orchid-patterned shoulders hunched.

Cheryl sulks. 'No, no.'

'No.'

Cheryl announces ungraciously, '*Gipsy Rose*, again.'

Pulling air over her shoulders, she winks into the auditorium. 'Imagine a shawl.'

The more experienced girls try to laugh with her. She takes four elaborately bored steps forward and gives a pelvic thrust.

'As you can all see,' says Ricky Vincent as if her thrust began his pep talk, 'first she presents *the character*.'

Cheryl palms her sweat-topped breasts around a bit and throws away an imaginary bra.

'I always like to motivate the audience,' he continues, 'so they're with the girl while she's building the number,' but his attention's nowhere near the stage.

Halfway through grappling a phallic shape, Cheryl demands sarcastically, 'Aren't I trying hard enough, or something?'

No one so much as chuckles. In their seats, leaned forwards, all the girls' gazes are intent on Ricky Vincent as he's drawn towards the door.

The GM pokes his head round, eyebrows high.

'He's here.'

In the trade, Pete 'Wild Woody' Harris' ability to produce a full ten inches on demand is legendary.

Ricky Vincent has to improve takings and if he's not going to go the pole dancing route, he has to at least see if mixed sex shows *are* more popular. Wild Woody in particular is considered a 110% sure way of pulling extra punters.

Wearing unostentatious civvies – jeans and T-shirt, pressed – he looks around, at a tinfoil bit of prop stage right, at the reel-to-reel at the back of the auditorium, at a section of gaffer-taped carpet. He rounds on Ricky Vincent.

'Is this the fifties? I can't work in these conditions.'

'Your pay packet will amply reflect "these conditions",' says Ricky sharply.

In their seats, the girls are a row of gaping mouths, except Mae, who looks cross, and Belle at the end, who is bemused. Square-jawed and small-eyed with a scar at the side of his forehead so made-up it could be plastic, 'Wild Woody' Harris looks oddly like her action man doll. Even his Brylcremed hair appears too perfect to be real.

'Isn't he handsome,' breathes Sue.

'I'll bet he's a vain bastard,' concludes Belle.

Sylvie laughs weakly, 'Will he be on with us?'

'With *me*,' snaps Sue.

'*I'm* prime spot,' calls Cheryl from where she's been left stranded on the stage.

Rubbing his hands, 'Girls, girls,' soothes Ricky as he steps into a shaft of light that adds flamboyance to his curls and casts shade across his face.

Belle's heart thumps against a seat-back she is trying to sink behind. Ricky Vincent's mouth looks unbalanced anyway, its top peaks unnaturally far apart over the plump bottom lip, but extra shadows threaten to capsize the whole thing completely. She has a sudden, thoroughly unexpected urge to kiss it back in place.

Staring hard at Wild Woody, Cheryl demands, 'Well?'

'All you girls,' Ricky Vincent announces, 'carry on whatever you were doing yesterday.' Then, on a whim, 'Or actually, the new girls may as well have a bash at impro-ing a solo, and,' his voice is sickly, 'Cheryl, *do* feel free to develop *Anaïs* if you'd like to.' Finally he's bellowing. 'AND I REPEAT: NO MORE SLACKING.'

Imo is sent off to make Wild Woody a cup of tea – strong, two Sweetexes – while he and Ricky get comfy on the gold bullion prop. Every so often, Ricky breaks off their talk to choreograph at his girls – 'Give *more* to the thrusts, Rochelle'; 'We've had dressed prettiness, so more naughti-ness now she's nude, for God's sake Sue.' – sometimes even leaping up to twist an arm or pull a leg in place him-self.

Belle had thought since she *is* more feminine under-neath – her body almost hairless – with the *knowledge* of her newly pretty poise, it would be practically amusing of her to wear an androgynous sack-cloth dress and knickers so chunky they look like boxer shorts. But now there's a real man on the scene, and one who's more successfully primped than she is. She longs to feel disdain for Ricky Vincent again, to be dancing the production number beautifully sur-rounded by her friends.

Centre-stage, Mae is doing crab position plus pelvic thrust. Sylvie's copying. Mae's hips go up, Sylvie's down, up, down, the pair of them linked pistons in a machine. In an attempt to do the same, Belle hurls her arms backwards, but she doesn't end up with all her limbs as legs beneath a belly table-top. She's straining to see where Wild Woody is with Ricky Vincent.

He looks *so* like her action man it's as if the whole world's colluded to play a joke on her, showing *this* is who she's been setting so much store by and he's come to life a plastic numbskull.

A reflex brings her to her knees. She tries to walk her hands behind her, cranking her body backwards, lower, but gets stuck in an inverted worshipping position. Wrinkling her brow, she pulls her hands away and drops, shoulder blades flat to the floor, toes in her coccyx until she doesn't even have the chance of a beetle on its back, which can at least wriggle its legs. Belle's are squashed beneath her. She tries to move her right thigh. Her left heel twitches. She blinks, and in that instance, her waist is gripped and she is raised to the correct position.

These hands seem to know her. They are firm – hotblooded. Real.

'*Now* try thrusting,' instructs Ricky Vincent.

Her hair sweeps the floor as she nods her head. Apart from that, she doesn't move. Her dress has slipped up over her ribs. Her tummy button is as high as it will go. It is a part so private that masseurs treat it as coyly as they do genitals, and hers is exposed.

Ricky Vincent's thumbs press in. His breath heats the pit of her stomach.

'I said, thrust.'

Blood pumps into her head, and pumps, and more. A horseshoe of girls tints rosily. Upside down they're smiling, which means they are commiserating.

Belle is about to collapse when the hands grasp and lift her. Precisely with the music's beat the hands release her, split seconds before oblivion, catching her and lifting, and release, and lift.

What need is there to know your body when someone else knows it for you, she wonders?

Ricky Vincent murmurs, 'You'll learn.'

Improvising centre-stage, Sylvie's skirt-suit creaks as she pelvic thrusts. Her smile is beyond her teeth, black holes on either side. Belle, grasping a nonexistent pole, has hidden her face in her forearms. Her dress is dust-streaked, crumpling at her hips as she shafts up, and down, and up, and down.

By this point if it were the real thing, not an impro, they'd be naked before an audience, alone. Only Mae continues with easy grace, casually chewing her gum as she palms her canary yellow boob-tube.

Ricky Vincent claps once. They stop, Mae solid in horse-riding stand, Belle and Sylvie teetering unhappily.

'Nice try, girls,' he says. A sneer fattens his lip.

Girls are drifting into the dressing room, chatting to each other, opening lockers, putting on the kettle for a round of tea, starting to undress. Sue, in front of a section of mirror framed with photographs of her baby boy, snaps the elastic band off her top knot and rearranges her hair in a homely bun.

The kettle sends out a cloud of steam round Debs by the fridge in just a T-shirt and biker's boots methodically squeezing out tea-bags.

Imo presents her face to a mirror. With a brown pencil, she draws a new mouth round her real one and fills it in with red glitter lipstick. She sticks on false lashes and –

anticipating the watering – immediately presses a finger under each eye, damming. Liquid pools in the far corners and then falls past her clown's grin in the shape of two perfect tears.

It may only be an allergic reaction, but it seems this is too much for Sylvie. On her central orange stool, apparently to her own surprise, she wails, '*A man*, when I was only ever going to go as far as topless anyway and now there's going to be *a man* with me on stage!'

'It's just a wind-up,' Debs assures the room. 'He's probably just doing a one-off Summer Special.'

'I hope so,' Imo admits. 'All girls is, I dunno, kind of cosy – like Ricky says, more *burlesque*.'

'Yeah, he's a real wordsmith,' snorts Mae.

'An ex-Peepland tart's more likely to bring the tone down,' snaps Sue.

'Leave her be!' says Rochelle. 'She was just earning a living like the rest of us. Anyway, what's a couple of hand-jobs?'

'I did *not* do hand-jobs at Peepland!'

Sylvie blanches. Debs starts another job application.

'All I was saying' – Sue's eyelids flutter – 'was I don't think it would be such a bad thing to have a man with Wild Woody's reputation on board.'

Mae's voice is bright. 'He is pretty hunky, isn't he?'

'Can't be your type though,' Belle ribs.

'Why?' asks Sue.

Mae kicks. 'I mean,' Belle gabbles, 'he's too squeaky clean, *too* hunky, too convinced that we're all in here talking about how good-looking he is. I *guess* he's not Mae's type, just like he's not mine either.'

'As long as someone with the right equipment is,' says Sue, her eyes slicing between the two new girls, who stand rigid side by side. 'We don't like dykes round here. Have to be careful where you strip.'

Stepping closer, Sue removes her top. Mae and Belle smile blankly at her naked breasts.

'I wouldn't like to feel inhibited.' Sue's eyes stay narrowed. 'Cos if I don't feel safe in here, it'd affect my performance out there, and Ricky'd want to know why.'

'No problem!'

'Strip away!' Belle encourages as Sue stalks off to have a shower.

Shakily, Mae begins the job of customising her mirror section, Blu-tacking up holiday snapshots of her male cousins.

Belle whispers, 'But you were kissing her in public.'

Sylvie admits, 'I saw too.'

Mae's voice is low. Her hands on the back of Belle and Sylvie's necks ensure that theirs will be too.

'I don't pretend I'm not a dyke. But I don't think it's necessary to ram it down anybody's throat either. OK?'

Mae's grip is particularly tight on Belle, whose nod is dislocated, her stare about to pop out.

'Fine by me.'

'And me,' gasps Sylvie.

Around the dressing room, the other girls' concentration is on their own reflections or fitting each other's headstockings or stirring tea or rubbing bodies with exfoliating mitts. Although still speaking as if through gossamer, Mae does relax a little.

'I don't have to tattoo the bloody women's symbol on my knuckles, do I? As it happens, I'm Tory too. I eat mainly organic. I support fox-hunting. But I don't suppose you frigging well expect me to go on protest marches about any of that, do you?'

'We're all different,' Sylvie exclaims gladly. 'My mum's a hairdresser. Belle's is famous.' Even as she is saying the words her hand is trying to scoop them back in her mouth.

Mae looks faint at first. 'You're a day-tripper, slumming it, for a laugh – *a laugh*, AT WHO?'

'Please keep your voice down, I'm not laughing at anyone, and that's the truth, I have *massive* respect for you, and she's only famous in her field. It's a minor TV show.'

Mae glances side to side in thought then grabs Belle's jaw and squeezes her mouth as if she's forcing medicine in. 'You have no idea, no fucking idea – it's not just your own debts but your family's too and some shit factory job doesn't even scratch the surface and you're spiralling – but I did it, I got out. I've worked *up* to this. Mummy could probably snap her fingers and get you a job in the *meed-ee-ah* tomorrow.'

'She wouldn't.'

'That's not the fucking point.'

Mae lets Belle go with a jettisoning movement. Staggering, Belle rubs where her colleague imprinted fingertips on her face.

Actually, Mae is quite relieved. She couldn't give two hoots about Belle's background. Allies are useful, especially ones with a vested interest in keeping their mouth shut. Belle has something on Mae; Mae has something on Belle:

it is the best way forward. As for Sylvie, Mae thinks she is a mouse. And anyway, if it does slip out beyond these two – Mae shrugs – her time backstage will become less pleasant, but she knows how good she is. Her contempt for the work fires her performances. Whatever Ricky Vincent learns about her private life, he won't chuck her.

Although, just for good measure, Mae tells Belle, 'You patronising shit,' and storms out.

Earlier, the backstage area was claustrophobic for being over-crowded with people and costumes and corridors turning back on themselves, but all the doors were at least ajar. It is nearer the show. Belle seems to have been forcing doors open for ever, bracing herself for a shower-room empty except of steam and smells of freshened skin, a cupboard full of shoes, all in a heap, heels sticking arbitrarily through T-bar straps like daggers through eye-holes. Another door opens on a cleaner's cupboard. Another door opens on a beast, crouched as if it was ready to pounce but noticed something odd between its hind legs that it is about to pull out. The way its shoulders are tensed and its hands are positioned suggest that whatever has been found is bigger, far more important than she is herself and Belle is about to witness something as momentous as the beginnings of a birth.

'Mae?'

She is in the act of pushing something in. Raised slowly, Mae's face sheens with violence. She smiles as the applicator pushes the tampon cleanly up, putting a bung into herself.

Belle bites a fingernail and rips to blood, eyes wide, unblinking. Behind her, Ricky Vincent is watching too.

Still staring at them, with a pair of nail scissors Mae snips the tampon string off.

To see this covert doctoring, particularly from someone as forthright as Mae Monroe, gives Ricky Vincent an especially keen pleasure.

'Time of the month,' he murmurs and slips an arm around Belle's shoulders.

She feels as if she's turned to jelly and all that's holding her up is the tiny bit of skin stuck to his concrete shaft of hand.

'Mae's going live tonight.' His breath warms Belle's ear. 'But don't worry. You'll be able to join her soon. Just keep working at it.'

Then suddenly he is a stamping prima donna.

'MAE, ON STAGE, TWO MINUTES; BELLE, THE BAR IN TEN.'

Xanadu's bar, halfway up the main staircase, at the curve, in a recess, is a feat of structural engineering. No one notices it when the grille is down. Now, lit, it looks celebratory, like a top tier of a wedding cake that's been wedged into the wall and has then subsided.

Belle is precarious on one of the two high black leatherette stools. She kicks off her sandals and grips her feet round the chrome shaft, but it is cold on her bare soles and she also grabs the seat with her hands, shivering.

Behind the array of bottles scaffolded upside down on the mirror tiles, Ricky Vincent's reflection joins hers. It is as if his face is being seen through water – hair fronding, flat blue eyes, lips at their most colourful and full – and if she reached out to touch, his image would disappear behind a rippling surface. The man himself, however, feels electric close beside her.

'Rick—' her voice sparks about the ceiling; she brings it low, 'Mr Vincent.'

She sees in the mirror tiles what she supposes he does, a sack-cloth mess with a Joan of Arc fringe-chop. Skirt yanked higher, she places her fingers in the suggestion of a bridge up her crossed, bared thighs.

This is the nearest Ricky Vincent gets to a coffee break – and it can't be a long one. On tiptoes, he's grabbed a bottle of whisky and filled the two glasses clinking between his fingers before they've hit the bar top. And now he's busy doing something else.

Belle's fingers sink. Mae could be more seductive in a bin-liner. Indeed, he has given her promotion. Belle envisages Mae dancing in front of her along a strip of chrome – live, now.

Even as her stomach curdles, Belle wonders with a pouty side-thrown glance, 'Is my progress satisfactory?'

'Satisfactory,' Ricky muses, tobacco pouch wrested from his back jeans pocket, lighting one he made earlier as he perches on a stool.

'Well,' he begins and stops to stare.

Head thrown back, from the upturned glass, the last of Belle's whisky drips, nectar into flower lips. Strained at this angle, her throat is so prominent with veins and lumps that it looks as if it is swallowing an erect penis whole. His eyebrows rise.

'Cigarette?' he offers.

'No thanks,' she says, banging her glass down and filling it again. 'And you shouldn't either. Cigarettes are bad for you. But in terms of *work*, what about these?' she demands, squeezing her breasts. 'Too big, small, droopy . . .'

'Perfectly acceptable,' he murmurs, intent as she drains another whisky in one gulp.

Slipping his pouch closer to her, he suggests, 'This particular choice of leaf enhances the flavour of the malt.'

Makes drink taste better – 'Then thanks' – and she grasps a handful of tobacco.

'You don't, ah, need that much,' says Ricky tentatively.

'OK, since you said I'd got it off good enough already, when *will* I be up there dancing the production number with Mae?'

Ricky deflates visibly. He probably won't get another five minutes off for the rest of the night. Brows hard down, he concentrates on absorbing himself in the pleasure of simply, honestly demonstrating.

'You have to leave space between the strands, to draw the air through,' he says, cigarette left burning in the ashtray as he moulds the air in front of him. 'Leave it quite loose,' he instructs while, eyes narrowed, she's planning how to smoke seductively.

'Then fold. And wet the glue.' His tongue flicks out like a snake's.

'Oh,' says Belle. Her heart beats faster, shaking her sackcloth, giving her away.

Ricky Vincent's face falls. 'Want a light?' he wonders dully.

And she pours herself another whisky, this one so generous it overflows – 'Ooops!'

She hoiks her hem to do the mopping as Ricky Vincent strikes a match elaborately into his body. It seems his cupped hands are on fire. Belle's roll-up gripped between her teeth is a straw, a very short straw. Fixed grin sinking lower and interminably lower, she is bent close, sucking in his flaming groin.

Ricky Vincent glances down impatiently as she coughs and splutters.

But after nicotine has filled her lungs, taking her voice with it in a plummeting death squawk, 'Hm', then, 'Hmmmm,' her intonation rises, a phoenix from the ashes. And she stares, wide-eyed, at the cigarette held up in front of her, a crooked, smouldering beacon.

Everything she sees is slurry golden. Ricky Vincent's huge eyes, eyes, multiple eyes are orbiting round his mouth within his cherubic curls.

He leans closer. She ties her body to the stool, lashing her legs, and still sways. His words seem to be wreaking havoc in the bar area, chrome strips, bottles, metallic reflections, fondant entrances tornadoing, Belle at its vortex.

'See you tomorrow. The auditorium. Three pm,' and he's gone.

Belle hiccups. She knows she is absurd. Yet it seems it doesn't matter what kind of state she's in, after each session, she is given a new appointment.

Between the scaffolded upside-down bottles and pouring spouts, she sees her reflection still fragmented in the metallic tiles but now she smiles.

It's traditional. The patient hands over broken bits of psyche. The expert puts them back together.

———

Back at Clover Court, Belle is deep in her terrain of drunkenness, tunnelled, her vision a caver's lamp. She has been spotlighting one thing at a time – front door, lock, key, left foot placed in front of the right – to get this far, sack dress hitched up, sandals kicked off, sitting at the chequered kitchen table, typewriter in its centre, her fingers hammering out ']=ksjhf[wythwkfbdxvoyw'.

Whatever she's getting going with Ricky Vincent, her *plan* was to be meanwhile applying elsewhere.

'Day-tripper' indeed – Belle thinks she'll show that Mae Monroe and day-trip out of Xanadu's faster than it takes to say 'glitter-coated G-string'.

'07tkbfcncvSGf;YIUgs,' she hammers, zinging the paper again and again until it is black with print. Then she pulls it out, swaying but satisfied. That was a start. The exercise mobilised her hand joints nicely.

Whisky followed by spritzers with vodka then rum 'n' Coke chasers was undoubtedly excessive.

'La-dah-di-dum-do,' she hums to bits of herself – arms, fingers, noses – as they split off and re-join.

One of the hands hauls the pile of newspapers' jobs pages closer. Another grasps the red felt-tip pen, with which she intends to mark her preliminary selection.

In capital letters, the newspaper declares, 'WANTED', 'WANTED'.

She taps the pen against her teeth, to keep co-ordinated. She scans the next 'Appointments' page. 'WANTED', 'WANTED', 'WANTED', so many they are blurring together. She will have red rings all over the place in no time.

In the hazy periphery of Belle's vision there are sheets of stamps, and stacks of envelopes. In preparation, from the ream to her left, she grasps a piece of paper and winds it in. The sound of the cylinder ratcheting is as romantic as a watermill, or an old weaving loom, or . . .

Soberness whacks her round the head.

Typewriters went out with the Ark as far as today's career moves go. Employers expect CVs to look professionally printed. Globules of Tipp-ex may as well be speech balloons declaring, 'HOPELESS.' And even if she doesn't make any mistakes, her keyboard's 'e' leaps, and it's not as if 'e' is an insignificant letter like 'z' or 'x' she could avoid. There are four in her name alone. Then, of course, to conclude, there will be her signature.

When her age hit double figures and she became a full *10*, she decided she had to become more adult and, naturally, she had looked to her mother, who didn't swirl her 'e's as Belle did in sheer glee to be doing joined-up writing. Lilian was so sophisticated that she made her lower case 'e's distant from themselves, prongs splayed: 'ε'. Belle had pilfered.

'Bεllε Gεorgε.' It took at least twice as long to write, having to stop and remember to be mature, to carve with the pen instead of doing breathless loop-the-loops. And now it looks to her appallingly pretentious.

At this rate, however, Belle won't be doing any signatures anyway. She hasn't started one letter of application.

She flexes her fingers and zings the paper from side to side. It is *too* clean, *too* white.

What is Belle to do about a reference? Telling her ex-Managing Director what she thought of him didn't make him inclined to help. A lie, or an economically truthful description of one's most recent position is acceptable, if one's previous employer will back one up.

As for how to explain her 'present employment', though, it's only a question of euphemisms. Glancing down the 'WANTED' columns, she sees 'Quality Compliance Officer', for 'snoop', and 'Regional Divisional Chief Executive' for 'demoted to the back of beyond' – lies that are in cowardly, smudged grey print. There is a great deal to be said for the full-colour up-frontness of Xanadu's.

And as much as she feels that Mae was out of order to be so verbally rough with her in the dressing room, she feels more strongly, indeed exactly as she said, a *massive* respect for the woman, not least because she took the trouble to speak her mind. Indeed, maybe Mae hit the nail on the head. Perhaps after all she does have a vocation, or at least a career she'd be excited to pursue but hasn't, she thinks, dared admit it to herself because it's the equivalent of the 200-metre sprint. She raises her finger as if it is a torch.

This work *can* get her where she wants to go. And as companions on her journey there's Sylvie with the face of an angel, and Ricky Vincent with the aura of a therapist. Xanadu's, Belle concludes, is definitely the place to build her life around.

Alcohol surges back. She rips her watch off and chucks it towards the bin – and nearly hits her target too. It feels as if rum's filled her eyelids. Failing to focus on the floored time, she rests her cheek into the typewriter's keys, and so shifts her head down the alcohol strata, vodka – getting fizzier – spritzer . . .

Ahead of her, the fridge swims sideways. Some kind of ornament is spiralling up, or, as she's seeing, across, a wiggling fish tail.

She allows her consciousness to float for a little while. She can worry later, or earlier, she smiles, since today has slipped back to yesterday. Belle's lashes brush gently past the 'e'.

When Belle wakes up to find a typewriter impaled in her jaw, she staggers up and to her bedroom, and crashes on the bed. She feels pain – throbbing head, acid stomach – and fascination at the way the wardrobe is somersaulting the window and the light's wire is elongating until it finally becomes a blindfold curling weightily across Belle's eyes.

chapter 4

*B*elle throws off the duvet and stands. Her body tips. She grasps from door jamb to door jamb to the bathroom where she presses her forehead against the cabinet mirror to spring it open whilst she pours toothbrushes from their red spotted tumbler, which she holds up ready.

In the past, she'd have seen it as a weakness to take any kind of medicine unless on the point of hospitalisation. But today she has things she wants to do, and she wants to do them well.

Spaced out on her bathroom cabinet shelves are an unopened pack of dental floss, an almost empty bottle of factor 25 sun lotion, and an historic packet of Disprin. She punches two tablets out of their foil packaging. As they fall, two trails rise and fizz the surface of the tumblerful of water.

In the hall, Sylvie quickly, quietly replaces the receiver,

before she's got through – although it is still a comfort to her to know that if her dad found out where she is he loves her so much he'd be down on the next train to personally give her a good hiding. She looks particularly child-like today in her fluffy pink house-coat and thick-rimmed baby-blue spectacles. She twists her fingers.

'Sleep well?' Sylvie calls.

A glass hits the sink. She sees a flash of silk paisley.

When Belle emerges from her bedroom, she is dressed in a tailored linen frock, navy with white piping, that would look suitable at Ascot.

'How about breakfast, Full English or Continental, your choice?' asks Sylvie.

Belle's arm shifts her along the wall towards the exit. Her eyes are hooded, her mouth movements tight. 'I've got to go and get a bit of fresh air.'

Unable to quite focus, Belle misjudges and gets Sylvie in a head-lock. Grinning, Sylvie wriggles into a position that's more matey. With her arm round Sylvie's waist, Belle's lips fall easily to kiss her flatmate's cheek.

'I won't be long. I promise.'

The bus shelter is a vandals' showpiece, smashed up walls, its graffiti graffitied. The seat is a thin slope at hip-height. It is especially tricky for Belle to negotiate wearing a slim dress, seams strained by braced legs that still aren't wide enough to give the necessary support. The seat must have been judged ergonomically sensible by the maker, the buyer; hordes of commuters use it daily. Because she ought to be able to, Belle could spend all day missing buses, banging her head against the graffitied wall trying to work out how everyone else finds the damn thing comfortable. The Disprins' fizzing has loosened her up. She steps straight on to an open-backed bus.

Even the vehicle's smell seems ancient to her, settling. Belle gazes up at the enamel panels, following their yellowed curve, feeling as if she is being driven into the past.

The empty cobbled street stretches forever, like a nuked city-scape.

Salt Way has always been unnerving. Belle doesn't look behind her, at the doorway. If there was a whole church attached to it, it wouldn't be so bad. But it is just a recessed, pointy arch, where litter gets caught and blown round and round, where Belle used to wait when Lilian had borrowed her keys and forgotten to give them back. She would crouch, her back pressed into the solid oak door, glad that it was locked, but knowing it was locked on dereliction.

On the opposite pavement, she presses the buzzer that activates the security camera. She smiles and along with the control panel's flashing red light there is the sound of the bolt being buzzed. She's in.

At the lift door, Belle stares impatiently through the pane of glass. The ropes curl up as the goods elevator clanks down.

At her dressing table, Lilian feels hemmed in.

After her daughter left, she couldn't keep the place as a shrine. She had to continue living here. It took many changes to make the apartment feel hers.

The sound of the lift docking is far away. In her bedroom, Lilian holds the brief for tomorrow's programme.

It won't take long, she decides. She will just read it through quickly.

Fingers raised as a visor, Belle assesses the living area. Every time she comes now all the furniture seems to be in different places. She wants to recreate a set-up that will signal to Lilian that this visit is significant.

Approximately once a month mother and daughter had designated cosy times that were witnessed by the man who came 'to do'. While he, with his silvery moustache and boiler suit, moved around the apartment – changing a dripping tap's washer, realigning a cupboard door – Belle and Lilian sat with cups of steaming cinnamon-spiked milk, half-watching a black and white movie on TV. Lilian would generally also sew, restitching a hem, or sewing on a new jacket's buttons more firmly, her eye on the flashing needle that was pulling loose fabric tighter next to Belle, sprawled a cushion or so away, homework on her lap, gazing out of the window or at the handy-man carrying out jobs they could have mostly done themselves, his hands building an invisible wall around them that over the years, the more he came, put him further away, mother and daughter more firmly in a glass tower.

Glancing at her mother's bedroom door, which remains closed, knees bent, back bowed, Belle starts dragging, first the sofa into the appropriate position, then the multi-drawered marquetry sewing-box in to close off the area round the coffee table.

'Darling,' Lilian calls from the bedroom doorway. 'Lovely to see you!'

A shaft of light pinions Belle, a gawky adolescent. Lilian's gaze is on Belle's outfit.

'You should use a professional dry-cleaners. Yours has bleached a safety-pin imprint.'

'Where?'

'At the neck.'

While Belle is double-chinned trying to find it, the sofa has been returned to its original position.

Lilian is in the kitchen, armouring herself with the sounds of tea-making, which is a precise ritual for her – kettle first boiled to warm the pot while pertinent china including milk jug, sugar bowl and silver teaspoons is arranged on a tray, leaf tea gently brewing. For Belle, tea is a hot, strong caffeine drink mashed in a half-pint mug.

Galloping after her mother, she calls, 'What can I do to help?'

'Nothing! I'll be right out.'

Now Belle feels like a four-year-old who can't stay still for musical statues. She curls her hair. She tugs it straight. She scratches where her watchstrap would usually be. She pulls a photo album from the bookcase. The leather cover and thick textured pages add up to several pounds. Crouched, Belle has to balance the album on her knees. And the delicacy of the intermediary protective sheets means she must turn the pages reverentially.

An early PR shot, grainy, of studio personnel at a cheese and wine reception shows Lilian two and a half decades younger, a career woman starting out, already stealing the limelight. Every turn of her body hooks the gaze. Her eyes and practised smile seduce the camera. A few shots later, Lilian's face is disconcertingly the same, the glittering expression reproduced exactly. By now Lilian must be quite heavily pregnant, and there isn't one full-length shot of her. It is head or head-and-shoulder shots only from here on until after Belle was born. And Belle is frowning, keeping her finger on Lilian's script, which presents a smoothly linear domestic life, 'Belle, three months', written under a baby propped up in christening robes looking surprised, then three pages later, the same baby crawling, 'Belle, eight months', then, further, 'Belle, one year', laughing and clapping to be standing on her own two feet. Except in the murky paper gaps, Belle is seeing the buckets of nappy sterilising fluid that Lilian said made her feel sick, the time when Belle thought her friend had phoned on her behalf and Belle got back the next day from a party to a chair smashing against the wall, mascara flooding her mother's cheeks.

One morning, Belle aged twelve went into the kitchen to see Lilian crouched at the freezer compartment, face level with its bulge of ice, frenziedly stabbing at it with a bread knife. Glass-like chips were flying everywhere. Lilian squinted and swiped at her cheek, surrounded by sodden towels, raging – '*All bloody night it's been defrosting, all bloody night*!' – both hands gripped around the knife handle as she attacked the ice wall.

Belle's voice was small. 'Lilian, mightn't there be a better way?'

'Don't you think I'm old enough to defrost a bloody icebox? I'm your bloody mother, aren't I?'

But the distraction was at least enough to make her change her tack. Then Lilian was sliding the knife in at an edge, trying to cut the ice away from the sides of the freezer compartment, without success, hacking with the blade – which got through unexpectedly.

Belle was running to her.

'I'm fine!' – Lilian's voice sharper than the knife dropped spinning on the floor.

'But you're bleeding.'

Brow ashen, eyes wild, hands cupped over her nose, Lilian commanded, 'Get me a clean blouse.'

When Belle returned, Lilian had assessed the damage – not too bad, it wouldn't scar noticeably – and dressed the cut with a swathe of bright white gauze. Hair tied up in a dramatic purple scarf, she had found a clean shirt for herself already.

'Get the camera.'

Lilian explained in her more formal TV voice that it had just struck her that such domestic incidence had so far gone unrecorded and perhaps her photograph albums could be more truly representative if one was included. Belle was listening, shaking, when all she wanted was to be throwing her arms around her mother and kissing her to the point of suffocation just for being all right.

Lilian arranged herself on the sofa in a martyred position, head thrown back – 'No' – trying instead a nobly suffering position, fingers to her bandage – 'No'. Belle's job was to put the camera to her eye and watch her mother from the end of a long, thin tunnel. Lilian settled on carrying on heroically, riffling through a stack of work papers despite her wound.

'OK,' she commanded, 'take it now.'

And the shutter went down.

Although, as Belle expected, the photo didn't make it to the album. In its place is a shot of Belle beaming on a pony next to one of Lilian gracefully receiving a trade award.

China clatters on the tea-tray in the doorway. Belle is rushing to get the album back, neat, to its place in the bookcase. Tray on the coffee table, Lilian is opening her handbag.

'Belle darling,' she declares as she removes her fountain pen from its embossed leather case. 'Naturally, you can choose how to spend this,' underwriting her confidence as she signs a cheque. 'I thought you might like a haircut. I have a new hairdresser. He's charming.'

Belle steps away from the cheque. In the high-backed broganza chair, tea-tray between them, Lilian's voice weakens.

'Please take it.'

Belle is apologetic. 'I quite like my hair as it is.'

'Buy something else – a blouse?'

Belle follows the line of her fringe with her finger. 'I cut it myself.'

'Or a nice smart hat?'

Sighing, Belle lets Lilian put the cheque on her knees, which stick out incongruously from underneath the finely watermarked rectangle of paper, scarred, bony.

'Excellent.'

Lilian's smile is full and winning. The fingers of her left hand balance delicately against the teapot lid.

'I'm going to try for a job in the media.'

Lilian's smile collapses.

'Probably only commercials, of course. But I've got it all worked out right this time' – Belle's voice rising with excitement – 'and I'm already well on my way to getting an Equity card.'

Lilian's right wrist arches beautifully as she pours a stream of tea. 'Exactly how? I gather they're like gold-dust.'

Belle is practically jumping in her seat. 'I've got a job at Xanadu's.'

Even the tea pouring from the spout seems to have turned to stone. Lilian's voice is a desert wind.

'As long as you're happy.'

Lilian's profession has equipped her marvellously. It can see her through – or, past – almost any situation.

In her new drive for a Mae-style honesty, Belle does persist.

'You know what Xanadu's is, don't you?'

'Of course, darling.'

'Have you been to a revue show, then?'

It is second nature to Lilian: one appears to listen; one smiles acknowledgment; one makes a link to somewhere else.

'One of my favourite girlfriends at college did a stint as a Bluebell in Paris. And Paris in the sixties was . . .'

Lilian's enthusiasms are real, that is her brilliance. She speaks of the Seine in moonlight as of a lover. The passion, particularly from someone so controlled, draws the listener until they are glad merely to be near Lilian's glow.

By the time Lilian rises as if, regretfully, this movement operates the final curtain, Belle is elated. The talk was shorter than she had anticipated. Indeed, it wasn't really a conversation. But that is because after all it was superfluous.

She's doing what she's doing. Lilian's happy for her.

How fantastic, she thinks, how extraordinary to have a mother so open-minded, as Ricky Vincent might say, so *modern*.

———

Alone in her warehouse space, Lilian is haunted.

She never looks at the photograph albums on her own. They are objects to be admired in company, a leather-bound, chronological set: This Is My Life – fame, glamour, good fortune. A snapshot now would represent the beginning of her 'growing old with grace' period, Lilian on the sofa wearing unshowy yet still flattering casuals, maintaining a relaxed pose, content to review her past.

Lilian's hand shakes as she opens the first photograph album. *Childhood*. Here they are, grouped on the front steps of the Knoll: Mother, Father, sister, the almost permanent house guest Geoffrey, and herself, young Lilian holding Teddy. The sepia quite accurately depicts some elements – the utility outfits, the bricks of their home – but it also taints the family's eyes and smiles. The picture looks sombre and yet her childhood was idyllic, it really was – pony-riding, orchards, village fêtes. It was picture book stuff, she was spoilt. She has never had it so good.

Perhaps her mother, 'just a housewife', had led a full life after all. That would be the final laugh.

Lilian presses her temples, hard, as if she might be able to retrieve discarded memories. She made enough mistakes for two. The album that presents her as a 'Young Career Woman' shows photographs of work outings and dazzling publicity shots. She fingers round them.

She was wilful. She succeeded, in television. She kept her baby when the 'right' thing to do, everyone said so, was to put an illegitimate child up for adoption. Things were different then.

Belle used to be her little girl. At bedtime, covers clutched around her chin, her eyes would sparkle simply because her mother was there, beside her, singing her to sleep. Now it seems to her that everything Belle does rejects her.

The apartment is bare – chewing gum removed from beneath the sofa, the kitchen sink never clogged with lentil bake, the living area's *objets d'art* arranged in their full fragility.

It's perfect. It's finished. Lilian feels she's finished.

She was a child herself, running with blinkers on, more and more often having to jump to compromise decisions, always meaning well. Lilian encouraged her daughter, sending her for extra-curricular lessons in whatever she fancied, and in some things she didn't.

The introductory therapy course was intended to equip her emotionally for anything. Belle was offended by the implication that she was 'bonkers'. Lilian was impressed that Belle managed two sessions. She could never do so herself. She was brought up with the stiff upper lip ideal. Belle seems set on beating it down.

———

She has her own show.

Ideas Lilian comes up with, for guests or themes, are spiked more often than not. She follows the researcher's agenda and voices their questions. She has to fight every new director to be allowed to do her own make-up.

In her dressing room, propped against her filing cabinet, the programme's brief raised in her hand, she scolds the researcher for grammatical inconsistencies. She has already kept Oliver waiting several minutes.

Flopped in her chair, Oliver examines his sideburns in her mirror then takes his pager from his back trouser pocket to check for messages.

Lilian can't spot anything else in the text to criticise. The researcher is glad to leave. Slowed by its metal arm, the door shuts silently. Oliver is comfortable in Lilian's chair, one plaid leg swinging over the arm, the other stretched out in front, polished boot up on her dressing table. He scribbles a note in his Filofax. His grey eyes wander vaguely. He doesn't look in the least annoyed.

Lilian does. Against the filing cabinet, it seems she is assaulted by the carmine red of her own trouser suit.

Then, miraculously, in her handbag, right in front of Oliver on her dressing table, her mobile rings.

Now he does look annoyed, his eyes darting from the bag to her face, which begs his forgiveness as she reaches across, her suit brushing his jacket, her perfume overpowering his.

'Calls on my mobile are usually urgent.'

———

Stickily synthetic in a Lurex halter-top and satin-style hot pants, Belle is running up the road that leads to Xanadu's. The buildings' façades are derelict, empty signs hanging off and on the ground. Everything is mutable – a market vendor who was trying to shift a barrow-load of button mushrooms yesterday is trying to get rid of star fruit this afternoon – but Belle feels clear enough to be cut and pasted anywhere and get the response she wants.

'*All right, gorgeous*!' calls a trader, gold teeth flashing as she ducks past and round a geezer street-hawking perfume, who wolf-whistles. Breathless, triumphant, she stops outside the 'GIRLS – GIRLS – GIRLS' cinema.

Against the wall, purse strings in the crook of her elbow, her clear eyes absorb the neon of the flashing 'XXX' sign, becoming red.

In the foyer, today's free-standing poster is a group shot, a row of soft-porn bondage. Authoritarian peaked caps cast shadow visors. Studded wristlets are raised, chained busts thrust forwards, bare buttocks back. It is precisely the girls' nakedness that makes them unrecognisable. Off duty, Debs, for example, favours lumberjack shirts and men's jeans. Her face is as elusive as melting butter.

Between stints at college, Debs earned cash with a circus, on a cruise ship and as a tree surgeon's assistant before she started at Xanadu's. She has danced 721 shows, all wearing shoes designed for glamour factor not comfort, and she's never so much as twisted her ankle.

Standing in front of the poster, she takes the production company's letter from her back pocket. As she reads it, her ankle folds, as easily as a piece of paper, flat to the floor.

Debs is on the carpet, one biker boot off, bare foot on her knee, her face serene. Belle wipes sweat into her hairline.

'Are you all right?'

'I don't think I am.'

'You're *not*.'

Belle tweaks her earlobe, adjusting her reception. 'Perhaps I can get you some ice, or help you to a chair . . .'

Grounded, Debs laughs. 'Don't tell Ricky Vincent. I've been picked to audition for a frozen pea commercial.'

Belle scratches under her top's Lurex halter-neck. 'To act?'

'I'm not going to be the bloody pea, am I?'

'Won't your ankle be a problem?'

'I've just got this funny feeling I'll be able to bear the pain by then.'

Belle's satin-style hot pants are skin-tight. She pulls a section. As air breaks the seal, her thigh makes a suckered sound.

'Congratulations.'

'Thanks.'

In the dressing room, below the purple ceiling, feather boas snake round shelves, costumes seem to be struggling to get free of their rails, the air is thick with sprays – deodorants, laquer. There's so much sensorial hustling, silence can be unnerving.

Imo enters under her headphones, two-stepping in her floral pedal pushers, gyrating her sporty bustier. At her mirror section, she covers the eyes of her reflection with thick false lashes.

Rochelle comes in from the shower, towelling her arms, and sits, elevated on a folded quilt. Quarter-length kimono draped over her shoulders, Argos catalogue balanced on her knees, she feels along the ledge for today's homemade snack, a box of hard-boiled eggs.

'Want one?' she offers vaguely, scrutinising an Argos page as she taps a shell against the Formica.

'Ooo, yes,' declares Sue, striding in with her son in her arms, nuzzling his neck. 'I forget to eat,' she announces, scrunching her nose. 'Weight just drops off me doing this job.'

Rochelle murmurs, 'I've got another half-dozen in my bag. Don't know what came over me. I brought salt too if you want it.'

She pops a tin-foil twist on the egg box and shunts it along the ledge to Sue's section, which is a photographic growth chart of her son, a mixture of Polaroids and studio portraits from birth to toddler stuck up round her mirror.

As old girls leave, new ones shift round the room. Since Sue has been here longest, she could have upgraded to Rochelle's place. She has stayed central. Sue's section is the first anyone sees when they enter the room.

'Hello,' says Sylvie, wrists clasped, brown eyes wide.

Sue looks on with pity as she sits in her seat at the wrong end of the hierarchy, by the door.

Belle used to be a woman who either wore clothes with lots of pockets or carried a rucksack. As she enters the dressing room the beaded purse dangling from her fingers adds a new sparkle to her gait.

Imo is helping Sylvie undo a stuck zip. Sue is teasing her son who is jumping up and down demanding, 'Juice, Mummy, juice!'

Belle crosses her arms, grasps the hem of her top, lifts and her top is bared. Rochelle licks a finger and turns a page of her Argos catalogue. Indifference flickers through the atmosphere.

Belle is neither disgusted nor turned on. It is just a body. She feels whole.

Imo twists her leg out and massages moisturiser into her inner thigh, calling, 'Sue, gimme a head-stocking will you?'

One flies like a kite tail over Belle's head as Sue strokes her face ruefully and takes out her Vaseline Intensive. 'Those spotlights aren't exactly Fairy Liquid on your skin, are they?'

In the centre of the room, Belle's arms are still raised. Muscles connect her breasts so tautly to her shoulders that it seems her torso is a halter system, secure even while her nipples are precariously in mid-air. Belle stares at herself reproduced in mirrors round the room. Here fragility and strength can go together.

Seated at her place, Belle grins. She has a locker. She has her own bit of clothes-rail, featuring a costume that was specially designed, *for her*. It is a collection of absences on a hanger beside her. She gazes in awe at the lack of shirt around a glittering bow tie fixed to a bib and tucker, the length of just a coat-back tapering from shoulder-pads, the legless formal trousers. And suddenly she's clasping the top hat to her bosom, eyes high. Maybe as soon as tomorrow night she'll be allowed to dance the production number *live*. And today is a proper dress rehearsal, full make-up and everything.

Belle seems to be rising ecstatically from her seat.

'Hi,' barks Mae.

Belle's face falls. Mae's is amused.

'Listen,' blurts Belle, 'I'm sorry about yesterday, nearly putting my foot in it.'

Mae's hand is hard on the back of her neck. 'Well then don't fuck it up today.'

'But I mean' – newly determined to be upfront, Belle shakes her off – 'can we still be friends?'

'Friends?' – at work? – Mae laughs out loud and gives a hearty slap to Belle's back.

Belle spins happily on her stool until the garish carpet reflected in the mirrors is swirling faster and faster, a merry-go-round blurring high around the room.

Mae straightens her shirt and crosses her legs on her stool in a yogic position. Her face in her mirror is a full moon. She daubs in purple eyes.

Leant forward at the same angle, Sylvie is shading her bottom lip. Parallel, to Mae's left, Belle applies foundation with a small triangular sponge. It is an intimate thing to be doing publicly. Belle is so close she can see where cream sinks into her neighbour's pores. Mae's pupils, seen from the side, are not flat but spheres suspended in radiating green. Her beauty is increasingly affecting, the core of her kept distant.

'Yours is a stage name, isn't it?'

'Of course.' Mae's top lip is only half done. Her smile is disorienting. 'My real name's Tina Ludlow. Hardly seductive, eh?' Filling in the rest, 'Mae West and Marilyn Monroe, one brash, both busty,' she frowns; that she needs idols is too much information. 'What about you? *Belle George* – it's got to be for real. It's crap.'

Belle thinks she sees a smirk across her colleague's face.

'Traditionally,' says Mae casually, 'skin-flick bods combine their first pet's name with their mother's maiden name. So you'd get Flopsy Baxter, or Thumper Hudson. For example, my sister would be Cutesy Kosta. It's a great game at parties. Try it. Go on. What would yours be?'

'We're not porn stars.'

'Oh yes, I forgot, this is just one big game of let's pretend,' Mae says, unwrapping a stick of gum and folding it into her mouth. 'Shall I do your bib and tucker up?'

'I can do it myself, thank you.' Standing, Belle slips the sleeves up her arms and holds the glittering bow tie to her neck.

The pads improve her posture. She is tall and proud. Belle blinks and everything goes hazy then in the mirror, her naked breasts come softly into focus, their sensuality heightened by the formality of the tie and collar.

Mae rests her chin on Belle's shoulder. Their clown's faces are the same.

The stage manager pokes his head round the door.

'FIVE MINUTES EVERYBODY!'

He is by far their senior. The girls treat him as their kid brother.

'Sue, your childcare's here. Better be sharpish.'

The imminence of the dress rehearsal is not welcome news.

'You look nice today,' he adds.

Sue is wearing a magenta skirt-suit. She blows him a kiss. 'You never say that when I'm nude.'

Out in the auditorium alone with Debs, Ricky Vincent has no choice. He must grant her sick leave. Her ankle has swelled to unsightly proportions.

The rows and rows of seats are empty. Up on stage, Debs stands on one leg, head bowed apologetically, hurt foot raised from the boards where bits of tape are peeling off.

Flustered in his satin shirt and paisley cords, Ricky Vincent bellows, 'SM! WE NEED SOME NEW TAPE MARKINGS, *NOW*.'

The Stage Manager is out on the back stairs having a coffee break.

Ricky kneels to press a yellow 'S' back onto the boards. Debs, looking down on him, says again, 'I'm sorry.' She winces elaborately as she makes her move backwards towards the apron's edge.

The ceiling is low and stormy. The festoon is a silver lining. A smile bolts across Ricky's face.

'Of course, the girls will suffer. You'll have a lot of others' doubled shifts to make up for when you're well again.'

*

In the dressing room, Belle paces, already outfitted for the production number. Mae is still in her civvies waistcoat. She's only just got round to taking off her knickers.

'Come *on*,' Belle pleads.

Last time she saw Ricky Vincent, it seemed to her that he had answers. She resumes her pacing, driving her heels into the carpet as she turns flicking her coat-tails, drumming the rim of her top hat.

Now Mae is sitting on the floor cross-legged. Belle stops.

'What are you doing?'

'Meditating.'

'Why *now*?' Belle demands.

'Quieten down and I'll be finished quicker.'

Sue emerges from the shower, towelling her hair down one side of her body. In a corner, Rochelle, half girl half *Justine in Leather*, is embracing a naked Imo, consoling. 'And *then* what did he say?'

The five-minute time-check was called ages ago.

Belle suddenly decides. 'I'm off.'

Cheryl is in the corridor outside her own individual dressing room. She is a human gate, bum on one chair, feet up on another, toes splayed with bits of cotton wool. Belle approaches skew-whiff, as if getting her bearings for a high-jump. Face over her shoulder, heels leading, her legs vault Cheryl's.

Cheryl brandishes her nail-varnish brush too late.

'What the . . .'

On stage, in amongst the back wall's jumble, Ricky Vincent is by the deco elevator, which casts bars that are more sinister than the prop's real plywood ones because if he moves, these shadow manacles move with him.

Belle is hovering uncertain in the mouth of the corridor. Delicate blue veins make her breasts beneath her bib and tucker part of an elaborate lace necklace. She tickles to make the nipples harden into jewels, pulls her top hat down, which forces her blonde wig out, absurdly bouffant, and she leaps on stage into the middle of a vast plain of light. She can't see Ricky Vincent anywhere. At a standstill like this, to meet the uphill challenge of her six-inch heels, it helps Belle to straddle her legs. Light reflected from her thighs flashes.

In the wings, perched on the green baize desk, Debs puts her finger to her lips. Belle wavers then steadies with the thought that soon *she'll* be the one invited to audition for a television commercial. And Ricky Vincent will help her get there.

Her stilettos strike, two drum beats, challenging him to emerge.

He takes centre stage on the victory 'V' Far beneath the grease-paint, she blushes. But by putting her hands on her hips and tensing her shoulders, she can harness her chest muscles. He laughs. Her enthusiastic entrance has caused chaos in the ranks.

Mae enters, stumbling and cursing Belle under her breath. Cheryl is doing an anxious heel-hop to keep up, yelling over her shoulder down the corridor, 'Come on. EVERYONE.' Sylvie scampers after, struggling to fasten her costume. The rest of the girls follow looking time-travelled – they aren't usually out here yet. Sue's still stuffing her hair under her wig, muttering, 'This should count as overtime, or *pre*-time, anyway, it's EXTRA-time.'

Imo and Rochelle, glancing round dazed, see Debs.

'What's wrong?' asks Imo.

'Nothing serious, I hope,' says Rochelle.

'Well?' Ricky Vincent demands.

Debs daren't look any of them in the eye. 'I *can't* come in tomorrow, I just *can't*.'

Rochelle's urgent – 'And what about now?'

Debs points desperately to her ankle. Rochelle nods resignedly.

'That's just great!' says Sue.

'Who'll do *First-Century Queen*?' cries Imo.

Belle's false eyebrows crinkle above her real ones.

'Cheryl,' says Ricky Vincent.

'I'll only dance *Anaïs*.'

'Sue.'

'Extra set, extra pay,' Sue declares triumphantly.

'For Christ's sake!' Ricky Vincent glares from truculent girl to girl. 'Cheryl, cover for Debs tonight. Sue, do tomorrow, and' – his voice becomes grand – 'I wonder who I should choose as understudy.'

Most of the girls step back, Belle forward.

'You certainly weren't up to it at yesterday's rehearsal.' Ricky Vincent sighs. 'I'll need convincing,' and he's clapping his hands together, his face thunderous. 'Well? Get going. Go and change. Boadicea. Pronto.'

Belle is alone in the dressing room. Hatless polystyrene heads stare from the shelf. There is no clock ticking, which makes the rush more urgent. For all she knows she is late already.

She wrenches her bib and tucker whilst shaking her jacket sleeves down her arms. It is easy to find the appropriate costume. It has been put in order of wear, at the front of the rail.

As Belle does up the final bit of Velcro, disappointment registers. The costume fits. It shouldn't. It was supposed to have been custom made for someone else.

Belle turns away. Almost any way brings her face to face with her reflection.

Many could fit the costume, but she is the one who's wearing it. The head-piece provides a visor in addition to her lashes. The bustier is flexible chain mail. It clasps the contours of her breasts. Her G-string curves over her pudenda as a codpiece. It glints and looks impenetrable.

At a front corner of the stage, Ricky Vincent is positioned foot up, like a gunman in a saloon whose enemies are all around him. His straight leg's a pivot. His finger is a sharp shooter.

He fires behind him, at Rochelle. 'Lazy!'

She is impro-ing *Justine in Leather* on the entrance steps, pelvic-thrusting a pillar.

'You're using the pole too much. Work with your hat.'

He turns to Sue who is doing the splits in the aisle.

'Yup,' he concedes amiably. 'Fanny to the floor – they like it. But don't overdo the stunts.'

Stage left, still out of sight, Belle lifts an ear-flap. There is noise, rattling from a 10-inch portable cassette deck, but the volume's low. The music is just to provide a basic eight count.

She thought she would get a special lead in, say from the GM or SM or some other member of ground staff.

At the front of the apron, Ricky Vincent clutches his head in despair. 'No, *no*, NO!'

Sylvie is failing to remember the production number sequence again, her coat-tails veering left when she is trying to leap back.

Ricky cries, 'Can't you just follow Mae?'

Chewing in time, Mae does eight steps, pause, eight steps, pose, in a roughly Union Jack formation.

'Come *on*. Present yourself!' he chides.

She blows a pink bubble from her mouth as she raises her arms, bursts it as she turns – in Belle's direction.

Belle lurches stage left. She flicks her breast armour, but of course it doesn't ting. Her nipples rearrange the fabricated chain mail as they stiffen. An attempt to march bravely forward is subverted by her stiletto heels, which make her wiggle. She is dazzling in the spotlight.

'Ah ha!' says Ricky Vincent.

Ricky is fed up – of being forced to consider hiring a man when he'd always thought mixed-sex shows vulgar; of suspecting Debs of leading him up the garden path, even if it is with a genuinely swollen ankle. He has judged Belle way out of her depth. She can't even take her drink.

Ricky puts his hands on his paisley hips and pushes them forward. He puffs his blue satin chest. She's a new girl doing her first impro. The usual thing is for them to try and impress him, get stuck doing the splits, swing round a pole too fast and fly off, something like that.

'OK!' he shouts. 'Everyone can relax and watch this one!'

The girls subside and lean round the auditorium, most wryly, Sylvie apprehensively. This is Belle's biggest moment yet.

'Don't worry about the story-line.' Ricky leads her in. '*One*, two, three, four . . .'

'One' takes her up to banging the low beam. 'Two' takes her down, head clutched as the auditorium seems to her to go drunken crazy. Seats flutter, celebratory streamers. Belle smiles. On the count of 'three' she throws her cape off. Centre stage, a bejewelled wristlet rises and her hand, balanced on the end, becomes a fist.

She has tape markings on the boards to tell her where to go, a beat to tell her when. And if she does flounder, Ricky Vincent's lithe fingers are near to catch her.

As she steps the eight count, the chain mail stimulates her nipples further. Crossing her hands behind her back to find the fastening heightens the sensations. And – 'Ooo' – what a lovely tickling the codpiece gives when she does some hip gyrations. She misses out the next eight steps to do this fluid pose some more.

'Aaaah.'

She can't see a thing above the boards, of course, since her wig and visor got pushed down when she conked her head. She pouts her lips. That's all her head is now, a battle helmet and a huge grease-painted mouth.

'*Oooooh*.'

As she does a swinging 360-degree turn, she shrugs. He

will tell her quick enough if she's doing something wrong.

She tosses off the bustier. Her breasts are a mass of nerves to be untangled. She does some manipulation.

This is all so right, so natural.

'*Yeees* . . .'

Her style's too actual. Girls are supposed to do suggestion only. She's moving to her rhythm, not the eight count. She's breaking basic rules.

'Go for it!' calls Debs from the wings.

Sue flounces her bridal train in the aisle.

'Maybe she'll get your spot,' goads Cheryl.

'More likely yours,' snaps Sue.

On the apron of the stage, Sylvie takes off her top hat to her flatmate. Beside her, Mae grins. Belle grins.

She's done it. She's transformed.

She hadn't expected to like the person she started to see, let alone admire her. Alone in the main spot, she is beatified. Under her visor, she's in a black and glittering dream world. She could carry on forever. She moves to present her final 'V'.

Ricky Vincent's walk away from Belle is stilted.

Shielding her message with her body, Mae thumbs over her shoulder in his direction and with her other hand moulds an erection. Belle's lashes hit her visor. She mouthes, *No!*

Mae nods, *Yes!*

Belle's head knocks the ceiling again. It doesn't matter. She has a helmet on.

The auditorium door opens. The Stage Manager peeps round.

'PHONE CALL FOR BELLE GEORGE,' he bellows.

'SOME *LADY* WANTS A WORD. SAYS IT'S URGENT.'

As the auditorium door shuts behind her, Belle glances left, right. She is definitely alone.

'YES!' she whisper-yells, victory punching the air and leaping down the central Xanadu's staircase, three steps at a time, four, five, and still not coming a cropper.

'YES!'

At the bottom, the foyer feels huge, silent as a mausoleum. In her silver cape, Belle twirls over to the telephone receiver dangling over the front desk, down the centre of its single castellation, the wire stretched by the handset, which is a dead weight, smooth as bone. Belle grasps it and leans against the cash desk.

'Hello?'

Lilian White replies, '*Darling.*'

It is as if Mummy has turned up minutes after her daughter has learned she's to play the Virgin Mary in the school Nativity.

'Lilian,' Belle whispers excitedly, 'I'm *First-Century Queen*!'

'*Really.*'

'I'm dressed as Boudicca,' she declares, 'only Ricky Vincent calls her "Boadicea",' inviting Lilian to laugh with her.

'"*Boadicea*".'

Belle explains eagerly, 'I mean, I'm doing the production number live in a couple of nights anyway, which is exciting enough for me because I didn't think I'd ever be that co-ordinated but that's in a group and now I've suddenly been picked over not just another new girl but over some of the experienced girls to do a solo, he says as understudy, but everyone knows Debs won't be coming back in a hurry, him too, so I'll be doing Boudicca in a few days when at first Ricky said it would take me weeks.' Belle blinks. 'It's a phenomenal promotion.'

'*I'm afraid I've had bad news. Your Great Uncle Henry has died.*'

'What?'

As Lilian gives the details, she herself sounds unconvinced that the news justifies this phone call.

Lilian's parents' generation has been dropping off like flies. This is the first time Belle has been specifically told. She's not even sure who Great Uncle Henry was. Up on stage a moment ago, she had been the sun, the moon, the stars. Belle's eyes are wide, the lashes prick her brows as she comes to see that now she must, she *wants* to put all that aside, because – she brings her brows down sternly – Lilian needs her. And she must need her very badly to ring during work hours.

Lilian's winding up, '*If there's anything I can do . . .*'

Belle fights to prolong the call. 'Was it painful?'

'*He'd had four strokes in as many years*,' Lilian snaps. '*By the way, I've found you the perfect job, it was advertised in the Times.*'

'But are you all right, have you got someone with you?'

'*I'll pop the details in the post.*'

'I'm coming round, right now.'

'I'm sorry?' Ricky Vincent is at the foot of the staircase, hands on paisley hips.

As Belle replaces the receiver, he swaggers close. He lights a roll-up. Belle's eyes begin to water, brimming kohl-black tears.

'Bad news?'

Throwing her body back at the mercy of the cash desk's bars, Belle warbles, 'I've been bereaved.'

'Unexpected?'

'Totally.' She raises the pitch of her voice.

'Someone close?'

Belle sobs loudly into her hands.

Ricky Vincent has had enough of the new girl for today. Twisting his lips so they gutter smoke sideways. 'Take the rest of the afternoon off,' he tells her. 'When's the funeral?'

'Tomorrow.'

'Tomorrow too.'

Belle peeks through splayed fingers. 'Don't you need me for the production number?'

He flicks ash to the floor. 'We can manage.'

But, thinks Belle, Lilian can't.

Outside Xanadu's, the street continues to be a fairground, shop signs big and bright, bulbs strung up round market stalls, happy crowds, laughter bouncing up between windows out into the blue, blue sky.

Belle is on a mission. She hasn't even changed out of her costume, just grabbed a mackintosh. Her spangly shoe-tips jab out from underneath as she runs to the nearest tube station.

———

Although Lilian was fond of her Uncle Henry, she learned when her mother died that grief can waste a lot of time. She also found that, having become expert at hiding sadness from others, she is uncomfortable with it in private.

In her apartment, in the bath, she is entirely covered by thick foam. She is chill at the neck. Numbed, her head hangs. The upside-down mud-mask's cucumber-slice eyes staring blank at the far wall.

This is the bath Lilian had always wanted, on lion-claw feet, white enamel curving up around her, brass taps that can be easily turned with one big toe to top up the hot water. The romance of it is too late. Her long soaks are not luxurious. They are stubborn, part of her conviction that there is a smell of middle age and it is rancid and cannot be detected by the person from whom it is seeping. Lilian stays in her baths until perfume has soaked to the base of every pore. Generally she reads current literature at the same time.

Today she is mourning. Memories bubble up, although not too far. She bursts them before they reach the surface.

Outside her mother's apartment, one of Belle's shoulders is braced slightly ahead of her as if she intends simply to barge the door. Salt Way stretches either side, thinner as it goes, sloping down as if to slip her away. She digs her heels between the cobbles and rings the bell again. The red light that indicates the bolt is being buzzed open fails once more to flash.

Belle rushes back into the middle of the street and – hand raised against the setting sun – sees that steam has stopped billowing from the boiler's vent, which means Lilian has finished her bath and is coming to the door. Or that the pilot light's gone out and water's overflowing and gas is filling the apartment round Lilian lying drowned.

Belle's fingernail on the buzzer is drained white and she knows the sound inside must be unbearable and she presses harder and she rushes back and stares up again.

At her mother's bedroom window, a hand framed in the sleeve of her mother's robe grasps the cord that pulls the blind down.

———

The sky is fading over one of London's smaller squares, its central patch of lawn scorched long ago. Withered flowers' stalks are propped by litter in their beds. The trees are as skeletal as the surrounding railings.

On one side of the square, Belle grasps two iron spear heads. On the far side, a building is under construction. Light only catches sections. The workmen are in thin air, each isolated from the other.

Belle's hair is flat, her head skull-like. Grease-paint is not designed to last. Its vibrancy is gone already, leaving her mouth and eye sockets gaping wider. Her face pressed between the iron railings is a still and silent scream.

At Xanadu's, in the foyer, the General Manager is cashing up, rolling £5, £10 and £20 notes into tiny plastic bags that fold into themselves like pillow cases. He lines them up behind the desk between the cashiers. The two dinner-suited young men lean back, loosening their dicky bows.

Front of house wasn't too bad tonight. They only had two obscene phone calls to field. It is bizarre that heavy-breathers expect to get direct lines through to the girls. The cashiers have to laugh.

'"Nancy Allbright" indeed,' one ribs the other. 'Mind, your tranny voice is quite convincing.'

'Nancy' camps it up. 'I've had *such* a lot of practice.'

At the top of the central staircase, Rochelle, Imo and Mae appear. The applause after the 10-11.45 pm show was almost worth an encore. Dressed in civvies, hems long, shoulder-padding wide, faces bare, smiling, they descend the maroon carpeted stairs, a grand amount of space between them.

'Well done, girls!' declares the General Manager, tossing a money bag from hand to hand.

'Goodnight, girls!' chorus the cashiers heartily.

The girls are courteous but swift, as always minimising contact with the employees who have contact with the pun-ters. Outside, perched on a concrete bollard, bike helmet by her swollen ankle, Debs is waiting. Debs is alternately red with the flashes of the neon 'Cinema XXX' sign and bright white in street-light.

'You jammy dodger,' Imo tells Debs.

'First round's on me,' says Rochelle.

They clap each other on the back.

'Coming with us?' Debs asks Mae.

'Glad to,' Mae grins. An ex-Peepland tart, she's unex-pectedly proud to be included.

———

Belle has wandered to the river, to Tower Bridge, a heavy 19th-century construction, two stone turrets bearing lattice girder swags, with the modern afterthought to illuminate it blue at night. Traffic crosses fast, drivers, passengers and even the vehicles themselves invisible within the streaming head- and tail-lights.

Belle jams her foot up and grasps the hand-rail. Beneath her, the river swells darkly. Her head and stomach lurch towards a barge that twinkles as it passes under, a party of bass rugby voices on board bellowing, '*Happy birthday too-oo you-oo, happy birthday too-oo you-oo* . . .' – and Belle sinks her forehead to her arms crossed along the bar high up on the bridge.

Nearby, on the walkway, a woman sits on flattened cardboard boxes, Special Brew between her palms, herringbone winter jacket over her shoulders, murmuring, 'I'm not doing any harm,' rearranging her sleeping bag, royal blue quilting over her knees.

Belle moves to sit beside her. But the woman is yelling, 'Get away, tart – this is MY patch; I've staked it. Bugger off. Slag!'

And Belle looks round for whomever she's addressing.

In the gutter, a road-sweeper brushing towards his dust-cart suggests, 'No trade here, love. Better move along.'

Belle's stiletto heels came off a while ago. The spangly toes poke up as if she is wearing jester's shoes.

———

In a bar, mackintosh buttoned up to her neck, feet tucked

right under on the bar stool, Belle has pushed her dank hair to look slicked back and wiped off the worst of her make-up. The young man beside her has just asked her back to his place. She smiles.

'Do you always practise safe sex, then?'

'Depends – you know – what the girl wants.'

'One-night stands too?'

Already edgy, he now seems only attached by his hands round his drink on the bar. 'Why?'

'Because just hypothetically, you could have conceived a child – you've got responsibility, you know. Because there might be some poor bastard out there with a bloody great hole in their life instead of a father – and – hey! Where are you going?'

'You're drunk.'

'I'm stone sober.'

'Then you're fucking cracked.'

'I was talking *hypothetically*! Please come back.'

Outside, on Geoffrey's doorstep, Belle goes on tiptoes.

This house has outlasted everything around it, disused railway bridge on one side, factory crumbling on the other. She stretches for the buzzer at the top of the doorframe and presses at the correct obtuse angle.

She ruffles the flatness from her hair. Geoffrey represents reason to her. Though it is past midnight, his studio lights are on. Goggles firm on his face, he opens the door, a bit.

'Hi!' Belle says brightly, straining past him into his hall.

His shirt hanging loose from his body shrouds the entrance. 'For Christ's sake, look at you!'

Her eyes and lips are puffy. She shrugs. 'I've had a busy day.'

'WHAT IN HELL'S NAME DO YOU THINK YOU'RE DOING WORKING IN A PLACE LIKE XANADU'S?'

Belle is stunned. 'Lilian phoned you?'

Geoffrey's body appears to be collapsing. It is at her level. He grasps her shoulders and he is beginning to shake her and her mackintosh is falling open on her chain-mail costume. His eyes gape behind the lenses.

'I suppose I didn't quite believe her, thought you were having her on, or even hoped if worst came to absolute worst you were being ironic or something other than THIS.'

Her cleavage streaked with grease-paint, her bare thighs and stomach too seem to her to be blurring the air around them. 'No, no, you don't understand. It's not table-dancing. It's not sleaze. We get paid. It's look–don't-touch. It's good, old-fashioned burlesque.'

His fingers are painful. 'You don't have to strip to get to know yourself.' He lets her go with a gesture of despair. 'You're too bright to be playing games like this.'

'You think I'm bright?'

'NOT WHILE YOU'RE WORKING AS A BLOODY STRIPPER.'

Belle is pale.

'It's late.' Geoffrey retreats into the shadows of the hall.

'It's so safe it's cosy.'

Geoffrey is perplexed. 'Aren't you ashamed?'

———

On the night bus, there are no shadows. Every empty seat glares, counting backwards to where Belle is.

On the right side of the aisle, the view is blocked by the driver's cubicle. Belle takes a position to the left.

From here, the forward view seems perfectly correct. There are the road's central white line markings, Catseyes winking. Above and to the side illuminated shop signs move behind as the bus drives on up the road, and as they go, new shop signs take their place, suspended outside in the dark. But then there are two layers. *Dixie Fried Chicken* is also *Kentucky*. They split off mid-blackness.

In fact, the view is an illusion. The shop signs that look most present are superimposed from across the road, reflections.

Belle moves seats to the corner at the front, where all she can see is the black pleats of the blind between the passengers and the driver.

———

It is 3 am. Back at No 12 Clover Court, on the kitchen table, Battenburg cake is Cellophaned to a plate and on either side are mugs, with sugar and cocoa powder already spooned in. Out in the hall, a candle by the phone is now wax melted to fill its holder and the wick is a charry wisp. Although, there is still life in the living room, movement all around – in the fireplace, over the settee, bluish, luminescent. The TV, left on with the sound turned down, has possessed the living room with watery electrode tides.

Retreating from the doorway, Belle pushes Sylvie's door

open a crack. In place of the shredded brown nylon curtains is a set with a dainty floral trellis pattern. A packing case draped with a lacy cloth is a side-table bearing a night-light that casts a gold glow around the room. And at first glance, Sylvie asleep in bed seems part of an Ideal Home advertisement as well to Belle, her blonde hair silken around her perfect face.

Except – Belle tiptoes closer – the counterpane is pulled too rigidly to Sylvie's chin. And yet Sylvie's skin is so smooth that it looks as if the sweat must have been dropped on from somewhere else. Belle is about to tiptoe guiltily right out again when Sylvie's eyeballs lurch beneath their lids and her lips let go a shout of fear. Belle is on her knees beside her, glancing desperately around.

Sylvie's rag doll is on the bedside table, uncuddled, uncried-on, pristine, its smile inane. Murmuring, 'It's all right, everything will be all right,' Belle tucks it in with Sylvie.

Then she swiftly goes for a flannel with which she cools Sylvie's face, so *so* carefully, to dispel the nightmare and still preserve her sleep.

'You don't have to worry, I'm here, I'll take care of you.'

And gradually Sylvie's face does calm, the violent flush diminishing to become rosy cheeks once more. Belle even sees the suggestion of a smile on her flatmate's lips. She kisses Sylvie's forehead before she leaves.

In Belle's bedroom, the central Bakelite lampshade spreads spider legs of light.

Standing naked by her wardrobe, she has brought out the blanket that her mother made. She wraps it round herself.

Its patched-together squares are shades of warming red. Lilian crocheted every single one.

Granny George said so. Lilian didn't deny it.

Sitting with a crochet hook of an evening, surrounded by balls of wool, tying herself into domestic duty – it doesn't fit Lilian's image. But then, neither did being pregnant, and that was when she started it – perhaps she had a nesting instinct. She made something finite, with holes in. She passed it on to Belle extremely gladly. Belle weaves her fingers into the blanket her mother made and clasps it tight. ·Nothing can change the fact that Lilian made the blanket herself, painstakingly, by hand, for her baby's future.

In her woollen dreamcoat, Belle sinks to the floor, unscrews the eau-de-vie and tilts it so far it is upside down like the bottles scaffolded to the Xanadu's bar, only without a controlling nozzle, glugging spirit directly down Belle's throat.

chapter 5

*T*his morning, although quite chilly, is bright outside. In the gloom of the hall, trying to peer round Belle's dark glasses, Sylvie feels fantastic.

'I had the best night's sleep in ages!'

Belle's grin is so big it threatens to split her head open. She closes it round a mouthful of paracetamol, extra strong. Her voice is small.

'Fancy a fry up?'

On the way to the greasy spoon round the corner, Belle downs a Mars Bar drink and only just manages to stop herself throwing it back up again. 'Reckon we'll be doing the production number tomorrow.'

'Reckon so, the whole team of us.'

'Solo soon.'

Sylvie's face falls. 'Solo soon.'

Outside Xanadu's, Sylvie suddenly remembers she has to phone her mum.

Stranded, Belle stares at pictures of nude girls-girls-girls, and Geoffrey's face is phantasmically with her too, disgusted. She bashes it away.

What does he know, anyway, she tells herself – he's hardly ever got more low brow for his entertainment than the Royal Opera House.

And Belle is struggling deeper into Xanadu's alone, up two, three steps at a time, hurtling down the corridor into the dressing room, where along the top and bottom edges of the mirrors, striplighting trammels round the walls. The fluoresence is thorough. Belle takes off her dark glasses and her head's vibrating, light thumping at her eyeballs – but it doesn't really seem to matter because, lit from every angle, no other bodies casting shade, without a silhouette to anchor her Belle feels weightless, floating in a chiffon frock, her breath a trail of frosty mist.

She is annoyed for a moment that the air-conditioning doesn't cool her vein, but then, she thinks, who cares, who will notice? And anyway, a new tic pulls her bottom eyelid at delicately speedy intervals just up to her iris, hiding the flaw.

She swings her beaded bag. Today, because of Debs' departure, she can upgrade her place. Out of the way of the door, nearer the professionals, she sits on her new seat, which is the same vile vinyl as her first, only less battered, its rip not bulging with disintegrated foam but mended. And in the locker is nothing but a sparkly pair of shoes, surely left there as a sign to her that she'll be following in Debs' footsteps.

Determinedly twizzling her stool, Belle clicks her purse open and takes out a set of photo-booth pictures.

At the tube station, she was the one who'd been reluctant.

Sylvie had dragged her in. They had to get their legs all tangled to fit. Belle's dark glasses stayed on. Sylvie did all the mad-cap moving, eyes goggling for the first flash, strained sideways for the second. She stuck her tongue out for one blast of the camera, pretended to be about to kiss Belle for the last. That got a reaction. Belle's hand went up to keep her shades on.

But now, to see hilarity framed as fact not just once but multiply strengthens Belle. Colour floods her lips.

Making the mirror section really hers, she positions her strip as if it is a photo corner for the larger picture that is a reflection of the mirrors' frieze. No other performers are here yet and she is surrounded by friendly faces – along with Sue's portraits of her son and Mae's snaps of her cousins are on Rochelle's mirror a studio shot of her mum and little brother and Blu-tacked up on Imo's a Polaroid of her sister. Around the room there are generations of relations with Belle right in the centre. She could almost cry.

Instead, false lashes fixed on, Belle braces herself for the initial blinking, which brings blackness down like the shadow of something huge about to fall on her again and again. Simply to resist the urge to duck is to toughen herself up. Over the course of five minutes or so, Belle has been reminded that accidents can appear to happen and repeatedly leave her unscathed.

By the time anyone else arrives, she is not only made up but with all her civvies off and half her costume on. Wearing the shoes and chain-mail G-string of the Boadicea costume, she is practising the crucial finale 'V'.

*

In the doorway, Sue and Imo seem yanked back out into the corridor by their eyes on strings. He wasn't a wind up.

Ricky Vincent is planning to put Pete 'Wild Woody' Harris on for the crucial last set. And right now, the GM is showing him to the performer's exit via a viewing of a dressing room – via what was *Cheryl's* dressing room.

Pushing Sylvie out of the way, bag flying over her shoulder, Cheryl storms in. Rochelle positions a chair between her own and Sue's. Imo pats her sweat-topped shoulder as Cheryl sits, flicking her platinum bob furiously behind her. Rochelle offers her a hard-boiled egg. Close at the mirror, Cheryl is swiftly whiting out her face.

Upside down in a corner, Belle is concentrated absolutely on her practice.

In the thrill of the moment yesterday, at the end of her impro'd solo she just sort of floppily touched her toes and thrust her arse. Today, the finale 'V' seems nigh impossible to her. She huffs and puffs to keep her hands on her hips to keep her breasts still pert while her spine goes against itself twice, at the base and between the shoulder blades, so her head can twist up.

For these unnatural bends to appear regularly graceful, a girl must develop supple ham-strings. Belle's quiver. Her head thuds and she's an ostrich, head in the swirly carpet.

Sue's son drops into view, apparently the right way up, because he too is upside down, imitating Belle's hopeless 'V', presuming it is a game. He laughs through his legs. She has to laugh with him through hers.

*

'So, Sue? I happen to *like* tuna baps with onion garnish.'

'Imo, you know the smell makes me sick. And no you *can't* borrow my purple G-string. It'd be the third night running.'

'*Don't* lend it then, but bloody well keep your kid out of my cosmetics bag.'

'FIVE MINUTES, EVERYONE.'

Out in the auditorium, even the rows of seats look forlorn. On the boards, tape markings are fraying off the apron. Overhead, the silver festoon is tarnished.

Girls are disparate. There's no music. Everyone is out of synch. In a nurse's outfit, Sue, down in the aisle practising a knee-to-nose position, looks dislocated. Amongst the back wall's jumble, Imo's *Gipsy Rose* pulls a shawl between her legs and gets it caught on the 'fiery' furnace. Centre stage, even developing *Anaïs*, beret at a saucy angle, Cheryl fails to appear enthusiastic about pivoting her groin around a fan-back chair.

Ricky Vincent enters and Belle thrusts her bust and flashes her glitter-ended lashes at him. She'll still have to leave early but he told her she didn't have to come in at all today. She swings the cape of her *First-Century Queen* self-righteously.

'What are *you* doing here?' he says and strides stage left to where Sylvie and a new girl are in tail and topper outfits practising the production number.

He's a busy man, he's just forgotten, she tells herself, that last time he saw her she was as far as he knew in a state of severe mourning.

Sportily American today, in baseball boots and shorts, he has on his shirt a chunkily outlined '1' motif – he's *the one*, and Belle is nowhere near.

Stare fixed wide, she speeds her way across the boards. Eight steps left, present an untamed queen; eight small steps right, defy the Roman invaders; getting closer with eight steps of being just a modern girl; eight steps towards submission practically at his feet.

Her body is so skew-whiff her legs seem to be pointing outwards, to thin air. Ricky Vincent has his arm around the new girl, whose top hat is precarious, whose left breast is palpitating. His lips murmur affirmatives in her ear.

'Excellent. You're building the number well – glamorous, fast, sexy . . .'

From where Belle is, head beneath her armpit, the number on Ricky Vincent's shirt is now a great big tick.

A voice inside her is yelling, 'BUT I'M HIS BOADICEA'.

She still doesn't have the stamina it takes for the finale 'V'. Her head falls and finally her eyes as well to see the five o'clock shadow that shows around her G-string.

––––––

The tube train hurtles towards the end of the line. Belle is alone in her carriage. She has already swapped seats several times. This one's no more comfortable. The address, on a scrap of paper, is stuck as a marker in the A–Z. On her lap the book slips rhythmically side-to-side with the train's motion.

Now her hangover has cleared a bit, she can see that

yesterday she got things out of proportion. Of *course* Lilian pretended she wasn't in. She didn't hear Belle say 'I'm coming' on the phone and when Belle did get there it was the time the school kids play their pranks. Lilian almost *always* ignores the buzzer then. And as for having to get her messages to and from Lilian through the PA this morning, naturally it was frustrating, but actually, Belle couldn't really have worked it into her schedule either for them to travel to the funeral together.

As the train rattles on, Belle rolls her tube ticket and unrolls, slivering with her fingernail till its edges blossom.

Grandly solitary in the back of a cab, Lilian leans forward to ask the driver, 'Is it much further?'

'No, ma'am.'

She readjusts her shoulder-pads and takes a tissue from her bag to catch the welling before it affects her make-up. Then she slots on her dark glasses, the largest pair she owns.

Arriving for a funeral service by taxi or cortège challenges mundane surroundings. Belle is a pedestrian. Outside the tube station, a man is selling copies of the *Standard*. A dog is connected to a lamp-post by an arc of pee.

She consults her A-Z. She is mazed in by privet hedges. House eaves poke over, mock-Tudor. It will be a good ten-minute walk before she gets there. A shopper rushes past, elaborately not looking.

Mourning garb can make anyone isolated. Belle is especially conspicuous because hers is so shabby. The pill-box hat looked black enough in the thrift shop. Out in the light of day, its veil clings like a cobweb to her forehead. The dress too is the worse for wear. She had to turn down the cuffs to make the sleeves long enough, and there the black is glaring. Because she has tried to darken her brown brogues with polish, her shoes look like blocks of finished wood. She clumps along and the skirt's pleats flash funereally.

Gates are high. She glimpses swings and paddling pools. She turns a corner and is running through parkland.

Summer is ending. This is a season of change. There is a gust of wind. It seems all the trees' leaves are dropping at once, every autumn colour. They are all around her.

Belle's eyes follow a sycamore plummeting. Her stare is swooped by a beech leaf, up.

To catch a falling leaf is lucky. It is extraordinary. Leaves flutter onto her head and shoulders. She reaches her hands out. They fall into her palms, piling miraculously high.

Lilian accepts that others too feel pain but can never quite believe that theirs is as acute. However, she appreciates the part drama plays in the grieving process. It is generally a help to have someone else to focus on. And since Lilian has had practice, she's glad to be that focus, not least because having a clear role to step into helps her too.

The church is a grim, modern building within a large car park. Lilian flourishes on the steps, greeting friends, relatives and acquaintances. Her dark glasses are glamorous. Her lips are vibrant red. Her hand-shakes are exceptionally warm. Her condolences are lavish. Blowing noses, dabbing eyes, mourners thank and clasp her.

Belle sprints across the Tarmac and stops at the end of the queue, breathless, no jacket, turning the A-Z round in her hands. Her eyes are all over the place. Her face is bare.

Lilian looks fabulous. Her daughter looks a mess. In this important sense, thinks Belle, everything is right with the world, breathing a sigh of relief even as she's hopping about as mourners continue to accumulate single-file behind her and the queue moves forward and she's getting closer to the chance of doing what she should have done yesterday – respecting that Lilian can't bear emotional displays. Today she plans to simply be here for her, showing her support only by her presence, and – Belle shuts her eyes to seal in the importance of this thought – she must keep her big mouth shut.

Yet when the black suit in front of her shifts, it's her mum she's facing.

'Are you all right?' Belle blurts and she's lunging for a hug. Her cheek is scraped by dark glasses hinge.

'Belle, you really needn't have but how kind of you to come. Why don't you accompany Geoffrey to a seat?'

Standing right by Lilian – *Geoffrey*.

Belle is ripped apart by rejection and is then a ball of fury that fizzles out to fear: what if he told her mother his version of last night?

Lilian is with the next in line. The exit's a whole car park's-length away. Belle escapes into the church, down into a pew right at the back.

Really, she's hoping he will follow her. And for a moment it looks as if he might, his torso slightly lurching. But he, too, came for Lilian and finally stays loyal in the doorway, staring into hands clasped level with the hem of his jacket.

In the church, white chrysanthemums stagger down the walls to the front. The air is bitter. One of her eyes starts watering. She rams it with her sleeve.

Every so often, she gets a set of odd feelings which, although brief, are so strong it seems to her that they could be real memories except for the voice in her head that chops them up by chiding – '*You're so pathetic*'. She's seeing herself a child sitting in a father's lap, or saying 'Uueergh' at his stubbly cheek after kissing him goodnight, or on his shoulders, the pair of them a circus act, only she's completely stable, ready to soar – 'YOU'RE SO PATHETIC'. She crashes to the ground.

They're only blips, but as much as she hates them in herself what she hates more is that she's powerless to stop them. And once they come they overwhelm her.

Leaning to a black-netted woman whose open handbag displays a pack of tissues, she wonders regretfully, 'May I?'

'Of course.'

Belle clasps one in her lap.

The pulpit sticks up ready for a vicar and a board reveals the numbered choice of hymns. At least here will soon be noisy – better than home.

She touches the netted woman's shoulder again. 'I'm sorry to bother you again, but do you think I could have some more?'

Every year, on the last day of summer, the caretaker turns on the heating in Clover Court. With a flick of a basement switch he links the flats. Neighbours huddle on landings discussing traps versus sprays versus dusting powder while, slowly but surely, water fills every radiator in every room, gurgling through as if the block is not a series of separate homes but one huge lair. Along the pipes come the cockroaches, up, over gas meter thresholds, through gaps in skirtings, migrating with the warmth.

Some tenants are more organised than others and lay their poison in advance. In number 12, Belle George's kitchen cupboard always seems stacked with it, in packets, cans and pellet form, ammunition ready, her fingers nowhere near the trigger when they should be but instead in her ears or over her eyes, still not managing to blank her senses.

And she feels as she did in the invasion when she first moved in, when one crept across the duvet on to her hand and she leapt out of bed to see that they were everywhere – living room, bathroom, hall – and she ended crouched till morning on a kitchen chair because that was the nearest she could get to the communal hallway without having to be in it, seeing if her filth had spread over her threshold into public view. Even learning later that the whole block was affected couldn't completely shake her initial conviction that it was just her.

If it had been the odd one or two, perhaps she might not have taken it so badly, since individually the Clover Court cockroaches are a stolid type, black and round like coat buttons. Their legs make them unnerving – they scuttle unfeasibly fast – and the sheer numbers of them. And Belle is too afraid to even scream, let alone do anything to stop them coming from the kitchen's floor-to-ceiling flue-like cupboards, all around her, *en masse*, legs hidden by each other's shells, seething.

Today, they meet with snowy barricades.

Sylvie's a bit annoyed to be having to deal with the cockroaches herself. But, she thinks, a funeral's a funeral and Belle has to be there for the family.

Sylvie spoke with the neighbours. Her hair high in a blonde pony-tail, feet in plastic bags in slippers, she snaps on washing-up gloves. In the middle of the candy-striped lino, she has a can of poison brandished in each hand. Any cockroaches that do manage to struggle beyond the barricades of powder keel, undersides exposed, and she's spraying so heavily that the tiny airborne particles accumulate around them as a flood. More hosing turns the tide and the roaches are spinning topsy turvy backwards, innumerable tiny legs scrabbling hopelessly.

Tissues clutched, Belle's tears play tricks on her, turning the backs of mourning outfits diminishing down the pews in front into a swelling mass of vermin and the hymns are the sounds of their legs and bodies clicking, magnifying, filling the church up to the rafters.

Belle can stick the service out only because she thinks maybe without the pressure of having to practically be host, Lilian might be more relaxed afterwards.

When someone dies, for a while their memory can be a life raft for groups of friends and relatives to cling to. Laughing, crying, they go everywhere together, from the buffet after the funeral to lunch the following day to a weekend outing in a month's time. Lilian considers this approach mistaken. And since she sees joint remembering as not a route out of mourning but a whirlpool taking everyone down, tonight she is busy, and tomorrow, on her own.

Lilian didn't mean her refusal to sound terse, her daughter knows that.

Outside on the steps, Belle stands staring for a while at Geoffrey. His concerned expression stays with distant relatives she's never met. No one notices her leaving.

Belle's wandering hasn't taken her far. She is still in an impenetrable suburban gloom. Street-lamps are dim and widely spaced, hedges are high. Itching, creepy crawlies coming at her every which way, she makes for a phone box, a beacon of light.

Inside, her face is washed out. In her black dress, she shivers. She holds her address book in front of her and grasps everyone she's known, all the surnames of the alphabet between her thumb and forefinger, and lets them free, a flick-book of deletions. Except, near the end there is a new entry.

Ricky Vincent gives all his girls his mobile number. He runs a family. They have to be told that they can phone him any time. Few will spoil their leisure time by contacting the boss.

Belle calls. He answers.

'This is a surprise.'

'You said "any time".'

'That's true.'

'Can we meet to talk?'

'I'm sorry?'

'Talk. About work, you know, the different parts I play –
I'm confused.'

'Sure.'

In his flat, Ricky goes to his utilities room and shuts the
door behind him. The rest of the apartment is chic mini-
malist – white walls, polished parquet flooring. Even his
weekly help is not allowed in this walk-in cupboard. His
domesticity is filed here safely. Electrical mod-cons –
washer, dryer – are stacked up one wall. Between, he pulls
down the ironing board and slots a pair of silk boxer shorts
over the sleeve attachment. He flexes his fingers.

Pressing underwear is tricky for him. It involves a lot of
turning so there are no ironed lines to indicate that he is a
fusser.

Ricky Vincent lives on a plush West London avenue. Each
side is a multiply pillared stucco façade. Neighbours' wealth
is expressed through arrangements of burglar alarms and
non-indigenous window boxes. Past the main entrance, up
four floors and outside his door, Belle practises a hand-
shake.

'No, no,' she mutters to herself. The action appears to
join two people in friendship yet establishes distance, an
arm's length either side. She simulates kissing cheeks. Too
contrived.

In his hall, slick in white jeans and a black silk shirt, Ricky
Vincent grasps the curls over his forehead and backcombs

swiftly with his fore- and index-fingers, and casts one last glance over his shoulder. He opens his door.

'Mr Vincent!' she declares and gives him a massive, earnest hug. He staggers slightly. She doesn't let go.

He rarely experiences his girls with clothes on, especially not such long-sleeved, high-necked outfits. Belle breathes hard into his shoulder.

To Ricky Vincent, the very density of her dress's fabric is provocative. He explores by feel. The weave is thick-ridged beneath his fingers, resistant. There is no easy Velcro. The fastenings are traditional. At the top there is a fiddly hook and eye. A zip curves the length of her back, its teeth gnashed right down to her buttock dimples.

Over his shoulder, Belle's face is very still. Her eyes are wide behind her hat's cobweb netting. His groin is pressing. She nuzzles his earlobe noncommittally.

Ricky Vincent sticks his arms out and drives her into the wall while he does some mwah-mwah in her hair-line that brings his mouth round to hers. He levers in his tongue and probes left, right, while his hands behind her ease the zip down, tooth by tooth. He reminds himself he's caring.

'What do you like?'

Chocolate? Chablis?

His lips are not so much cupid's bows as hunters'.

'What do you *like*?'

Sunshine? Flower-filled meadows?

'What are you saying?'

'Tell me what turns you on and I'll do it' – he lunges; she shoves.

'No lovebites!'

'So coy?'

'I'm a performer.'

'Oh yes –' then – what the hell – trouser flies undone, he's grabbed her hand and is indicating the rhythm with a couple of preliminary thrusts.

Her looped fingers oblige with *one* two three, *one* two three, up and down the shaft, her hand movement almost balletic, apparently effortless. Her head is leaned over his, a seismograph. She keeps the speed even.

His quaking begins. She does S-L-O-W, S-L-O-W, *quick*. His head is thrown back, signalling eruption.

He buries his face in her and holds her tight. He needs her. She clings.

He extricates himself and looks down. His trousers, pulled up quickly, are pristine. Goo strings between her fingers.

He says, 'The bathroom's across the hall.'

He is clutching a glass and a bottle of vodka that is frosted from the freezer when she emerges, clean.

'I've ordered you a cab.'

'Is that it?'

'You want a drink before you go or something?'

His eyes are hard-boiled eggs with irises painted on. His mouth is sliver cuts of sirloin steak.

She backs away.

In a nightclub south of the river, in the middle of a dance floor, Mae's lover yells through the disco beat, 'I WANT YOU.'

Mae draws her close, mouth-to-mouth. Their hands swing each other's hips.

'I'M YOURS.'

Way out east, in a tower block on the 13th floor, Sue wraps her son in her arms. She murmurs, 'I'm here.' He clasps her tight, a pint-sized comforter. Then he plumps her arm into a better pillow position and together they drift back into sleep.

At a late-night off-licence that is pungent with the pheromones of its owner's Alsatian dog, the back wall of shelves is mainly bare except for a stack of Thunderbird arranged like a target that has just been hit. Belle is walking out with one, the bottle wrapped not only in a brown paper bag, but also in her pill-box hat.

She is doing a dot-to-dot home, proceeding by bus stops. The street-light is treacly orange, as unreal and sticky as the Thunderbird she is swigging periodically. Despite her rock-steady brogues, her progress is slurry as she goes from paving stone to paving stone, avoiding the cracks as she did through childhood in case a bear should leap out, claws extended. The paving stones are large, some cracked themselves. She leaps two and teeters on one leg.

A man crosses to the other side of the street. He stands blankly, a silhouette before a lit-up launderette.

It is 2 am. She is at a junction. The banks of traffic lights account for a complicated filter system. There are hardly any cars. Currently, every single light is green, arrows pointing all directions. Belle can go anywhere she wants. She swigs the Thunderbird and continues home.

Swaying in her hall, Belle is not sure if she's relieved or disappointed or plain mistaken. She raises the bottle in her hand. The word 'Thunderbird' swirls but stays legible. She stares at the floor, her own head swirling, and sees just knots and splinters across the boards.

She tiptoes down and peers around the doorway. Sylvie looks peacefully asleep in bed. The place is not awash with cockroaches. Perhaps, Belle thinks, she got the day wrong – in which case, they're still to come.

She spends all night sitting in a chair, knees up, her head cricked in a corner.

chapter 6

———

*B*elle was once given a snow-shaker that contained a London scene. Perhaps one of the taller rectangles was supposed to represent Big Ben and one of the longer ones Buckingham Palace. It was unclear, and to Belle irrelevant. The scene was compacted. It fitted into the palm of her hand. She wrapped her fingers round and shook. The sturdy, geometric shapes vanished in a swirl of white. The orb became senseless. But then, after a while, contained by plastic, the storm did settle and she could hold her small, neat version of London again.

Her hands seem cupped for it outside in the street as her eyes go wild between a market stall tipping to merge its contents with a barrow display of rows and rows of watches telling different times. Voices of traders, mobiles, walkie-talkies, call girls, clippers all whirl round her, white noise, as if the world has been shaken and there is no limiting Perspex. She makes a dash for the foyer.

She'd been coming to feel that Xanadu's was her own, bigger than real-life snow-shaker. Creeping up the main staircase, the inside still looks the same – no windows so not a chink of sun to fade, immutable fluorescence – but she can't feel solidly contained.

Last night, she gave the boss a hand-job, a second rate one too, and the lack of phone call firing her, she's convinced, can mean only that he plans to make the humiliation worse by sacking her in front of all her workmates.

It's 6.35 pm. Backstage, the Stage Manager is rushing down a corridor with new stockings, chased by a carpenter yelling, 'Do you want this cartwheel fixing for tonight's show or what?' past the General Manager who's at the noticeboard with tonight's running order, girls jostled tight round him even before he's got the first drawing pin up.

The group is a wall of flesh to Belle, who is still dressed top to toe in civvies. But then Ricky Vincent's voice is booming round a corner – 'GM! I WANT THE SM, *NOW*!' – and Belle is pressing herself deep in with the Zone Fantastica girls.

Ricky Vincent looks at his watch as he strides by with Wild Woody. 'This is *very* inconvenient.'

'You want me as gaoler for the Queen in the Tower set as well,' Wild Woody says airily. 'I can rehearse now.'

'CHERYL!'

Belle steps forward.

'Hi,' says Ricky Vincent as if less than nothing happened. '*CHERYL!*'

'She's in the shower,' says Sue.

'Well tell her to get out, and' – Ricky is agog at the half-circle of girls staring back at him – 'the running order's up, why aren't you in costume?'

'Everybody?' wonders Belle.

'NOW!'

In the dressing room, Belle clasps the costume to her. She caresses her cheek with the satin thigh stripe. She gazes at the glitter of femininity the bow tie casts over her hand as she holds the hanger up before her.

'But what about *this*?' she cries at her stubble.

'No worries,' says Mae, giving a squirt of foundation to Belle's neglected pubic area.

And it doesn't take much porcelain cover-up before Belle can look in the mirror and see her thighs as smooth as a doll's either side of a black line so thin and neat she could be an item from a production line.

'GENERAL CALL,' the SM shouts.

The general call takes place on stage precious moments before the punters arrive to possess the auditorium. Each evening, one girl stands out as special – whoever has been chosen to perform the first set.

Wearing the frontless wedding gown, tonight Sue flounces her lace train centre stage. Her heavily beaded G-string bulges as if it must contain an extra organ, making Sue look like a hermaphrodite bride surrounded by a host of grooms, their breasts plump beneath bow ties.

Ricky Vincent, of course, is master of ceremonies,

standing on the apron's edge, hands on hips, haloed beneath the silver festoon.

'Stand where you like,' he calls generously.

The light is so harsh that it is possible to see details such as shaving scabs on shins. His gaze is on their faces, which are purple splodge eyes and red glitter mouths, everything else whited out.

Belle edges forward. Ricky addresses a top hat at random.

'Sylvie, you're progressing excellently.'

He slaps the back of his hand into his palm as he makes his proclamations. 'Imo, remember with *strip* there's *tease*. But otherwise, I like your *Gypsy Rose*. Rochelle, ditto.'

Belle strains her lids to make the false lashes far from her real blue eyes. Ricky Vincent addresses another wig.

'Mae. Do you feel a hundred per cent clear about your set? Just remind me how you'll build the number.'

'First I present the *character* . . .'

'. . . making it contrast with the preceding act's. Continue.'

Belle is jiggling her naked breasts quite madly now.

'Stop it!' hisses Imo.

'Yeah, you'll get your turn,' teases Rochelle.

But the voice in Belle's head that was just haunting at first – 'of course you're special' – is getting louder – '*You got promoted*'.

'Catherine of Aragon is soft when she is dressed, she is feminine.' Ricky Vincent is waxing lyrical towards the ceiling. 'She is captive. And so the storyline is this: there is a woman; there is a man . . .'

'And then he fucks her,' mutters Belle.

Over the auditorium, false lashes are falling. Sylvie

staggers slightly as if perhaps she has concussion. 'It's a solo! There's no fucking!'

'There will be now we've got Wild Woody,' smirks Rochelle.

Sue wants her star turn to be in Xanadu's the West-End revue. 'It's practically *poetic*,' she flares in the aisle. 'We're *choreographed* all the way to the finale "V"' – the thought of the shape apparently so strong her body drops into it.

The seats are a speechless congregation. Legs taut, arse in the air, the crack between Sue's buttocks is suspended, prettily framed within tumbling white bridal gown, ready for the onlooker.

Upright again, her neck is purple. 'See? Not just anyone can do that,' she says.

'See?' Sylvie repeats forlornly.

'It's burlesque.' Mae chews her gum crossly.

Whatever the spats before, once the show's about to start the girls have to be united or the night can be hard to get through. Belle has shut her real eyes. Her grease paint ones gape thickly.

Mae insists, 'Go on, tell her, Mr Vincent.'

His head is in his hands. Cheryl's busy with Wild Woody. Ricky needs Belle to bulk out the production number. He visualises first her soiled mourning dress then a percentage of the ticket sales. He looks up smiling.

'Wild Woody is of course *part* of the poetry. Every one of you is exotic, glamorous, fast . . .'

As he spins his aural candyfloss, Belle's breasts continue to palpitate beneath her bib and tucker but her eyes gradually open. Her top hat is at a rakish angle. But she is still a hermaphrodite groom.

Ricky Vincent's shout blasts louder than shotguns.

'SO? PERFORM OUR SHOW. *DO IT!*'

Belle can't believe she's not only still here but now in the dip directly behind the stage, part of the golden constellation that marks the beginning of the show, surrounded so closely by her workmates that every bit of her is touched. Beyond the stage, beyond the separating curtain, the mildly amused male voice fills the auditorium.

'ARE YOU READY, LADIES AND GENTLE-MEN . . .'

Only, it's hard to make the words out over the sound of the fire curtain cranking up. Belle strains to hear.

'. . . FOR YOUR EYES ONLY . . .' and the girls are pushing and shoving each other up to the stage as the silver festoon rises.

As well as the basics – making flawed skin look perfect with mauve gels – and the more entertaining creative elements – giving Ricky Vincent tinted 'moods' – the lighting technician puts a lot of care into making the girls comfortable, not for Xanadu's profits but because he assumes that the performers too ended up here by default. In his heyday, he was a Cossack dancer, one of this country's immigrant greats. His wife, his partner, died. He hates mornings. He wanted to stay in the theatre.

No member of staff who works in the auditorium is allowed to mix with the girls. He wouldn't want to be an exception. He doesn't see their bodies any more. He wishes he didn't know their eyes, desperate for something to focus on other than the audience. New girls learn before the end of their first production number not to look into the follow spot. It doesn't take them long to find the gaps he has left for them between spotlights in the ceiling, two blank, black spaces to buoy them until they are finished.

But Belle's here *for* the spotlight. She stares straight at the main one and it burns directly on her eyeballs, dazzling, disorienting.

It's a good job she is touched so closely by her Zone Fantastica associates, led blind as she twirls her silver-topped cane, eight steps left, eight steps right at the start of a roughly Union Jack formation, and her arms go up and her whole self twists, and how excellent, she thinks, that just as it was in rehearsal now, live, her body knows the moves automatically, no concentration necessary, which leaves her mind free. And soon her sight is too.

The burning in her eyes has diffused enough by the fourth set of eight steps for her to see one of her breasts flap like a flannel.

In time with the electro beat, pushed along with the others, she twirls her hat as she eight-steps up stage, down, thighs chafing on her pube stubble. She was supposed to be demarcated absolutely by now, a picture-perfect girl, femi-nised – and she is dressed up as a man.

In time, she flicks her tails. The top hat feels leaden on her head and the line-up turns and her false lashes are leaden too and she can't see further than the first few rows, which are empty, so instead of hordes of adoring members of the public she feels she's being watched by one huge eye, and not even an eye whose gaze she can meet and challenge but an eye that is hidden while it sees her through a vast dark screen.

A silver-topped cane pokes in her back and through her earth-shattering electro beat a workmate's voice insists, 'LEFT, GODDAMIT – BEND!'

Her hand is grabbed and she is filed from the centre of the stage without – her red glitter mouth turns to plead – applause.

And they've forced her past the first taped marker on the boards, the blue, the yellow, and the music is in the less abrasive thrash-guitar phase that indicates another set is due to start and, still being filed, the light of the dressing rooms' corridor now visible ahead, Belle has someone else's shoulder blades in front, breasts tickling her from behind as she comes to think to herself that *of course* there's no clapping after the production number because it's just the fanfare introduction to the show as a whole – she'll get her applause when she does her solo.

The Stage Manager's hand is across the dressing-room doorway. Belle ducks down. It drops with her. Her face is straining to be in with Mae and all the others.

'I have to change,' she explains urgently.

She pushes. The SM grasps her shoulder and folds her to the outside of the door jamb.

'I'm *Boadicea*.'

'Tomorrow, maybe.'

*

The linking passageways of the backstage warren converge to send performers down the institution-yellow corridor to the three steps, where girls pause lest they trip, seconds away from being on stage. Belle sits at this junction, her torso in with the props, her legs dangling in the stairwell on the border to the auditorium.

Her stomach is crumpled. Her breasts are elongated beneath the bib and tucker. The air-conditioning blasts particularly strongly here. It has reduced her. She is cold and thin, except for the vein under her eye, which is going mad. The tic can't cover it. Even the grease-paint is not enough to distract from its throbbing arc of red.

As if to mock, her top hat is stuck on her wig. It doesn't fall off her hanging head. She can hear performers whooping as if they are about to start a carnival. Bouncing round lockers and air ducts, their joy reaches Belle magnified. The stage is an aurora borealis, millions of shattered rainbows with Ricky Vincent on the other side. On top of everything else, Belle cheeked him in the general call.

He is practised. His staff are loyal. On the far side of the stage, Ricky won't so much as glance in her direction. The SM stands by Belle, legs wide, arms crossed, face unforgiving.

Belle kicks her stiletto heels against the stairwell. Two girls are coming down the corridor, hands keeping their headdresses in place, fluttering bits of costume dusky wings behind them. Belle perks up. She is ready if they need her.

She goofed the production number. Bare hands, sides, thighs pass her coldly.

The SM tells her, 'You have to leave now, the back way.'

Wild Woody passes her going the other way, deeper in to Xanadu's, to say hello.

When Wild Woody appears in the girls' dressing-room doorway, Sue is ingratiating. 'Proud to have you on board.'

'How-ya-doin'?' mumbles Imo before whispering to Sylvie that he looks like a great hulking ape and how can a monkey be a serious threat to anyone?

After her first solo, Rochelle goes out on a snack run and trips. Back in the dressing room, she has to incorporate a knee bandage into *Justine in Leather*. Imo spills Coca-Cola all over her *Gypsy Rose* shawl while she is trying to write a letter of application for a job as a waitress.

On stage, Cheryl's eyes are down.

The music cuts and the main spot has thrown her into a clumsy pirouette before splitting into two taut mini-spots that keep her chest high, leaving her legs to splay. Her hands danglingly hit her inner thighs, which are carved with grooves that take her fingertips upwards.

———

All the way back, Belle is calculating where the others must have got to – saucy maid set, explicit S&M, pre-interval two-some tantaliser – the running order as comforting to her as the predictability of door numbers on houses down a street – 2, 4, 6, 8 – three-some energiser, sultry seductress set; only, instead of being up there with them – 3, 5, 7, 9 – Belle is walking up the path to Clover Court, where missing screws and graffiti make door numbers go arbitrarily – 2, 34, 3, 538.

She's been getting in at night, coming out during the day. And now it's dusk and she can see quite clearly and it seems impossible to her that the block could have ever launched itself in her imagination as a cruise ship. Not much of its 1930s' smooth façade is left in place. A child has wedged a fallen piece in a grate where he is crouched over a game of marbles. From a ground-floor window, a net curtain billows through a broken pane. And people too are looking strange to her, a suited woman carrying shopping bags standing aside, carriers snatched back as if Belle was not gesturing to help but trying to take them.

Rubbish from the street has been blowing in through the communal doorway and accumulating round the edges of the entrance hall. A sweet wrapper across a crack seems to be all that's plastering it together. The extent of the dilapidation suggests that the building should collapse, particularly given a central stairwell that is such a yawning hole. Belle ascends gingerly.

Then out of the blue, 'Hi, there,' drops down like a rope. 'Hello!' she calls eagerly, no idea who to, clambering faster, tossing up courtesy in return, 'Good afternoon – coming in quite nippy, isn't it?'

She turns a corner. The stairwell's thin window has trapped in its wiry re-inforcements a ten-storey shaft of day, lighting up the speaker, who is on the landing by her door. He is dusty and dishevelled yet even the rips in his T-shirt seem upturned. Where his soles are coming away from their leather uppers, the gaps form two great big goofy grins for him to stand on. He looks to her like someone from a fairy-tale, his profile oddly flat, as if planed to have minimum structural weaknesses.

'Hi,' she says again.

And through a split second a story has bloomed in her head in which she never worked strange Xanadu hours and so bumped into him before and she can tell from the lines' positions on his face, fanning from his eyes, that there'd have been laughter, and empathy is etched across his brow.

The man's head and that of the angle-poise in the packing case he is carrying bob simultaneously.

Neck flushed, her fists go in her pocket. 'But you're moving out.'

'Only within the area.' Low, his voice seems to her to be teasing her to catch it.

'Then how about a coffee?' she suggests, indicating her flat's front door.

It was his advice Sylvie asked about the cockroaches. He's been in already. Elbow jammed between his hip and the wall to bear the weight of the box, he shifts away.

'Or perhaps a nightcap,' Belle pursues.

And he's shifting faster, further down the steps.

She's ready to walk on air. He's paused.

'You'll be seeing your flatmate?'

'Guess so.'

'Tell her I said goodbye, I'm sorry I missed her but I'll be round for her.'

And the soles of the shoes of the man who used to live next door echo down the stairwell.

After the initial swarm, there are always stragglers. Inside

Belle's flat, the kitchen is especially bad, its candy-striped lino littered with corpses. The piles of powder that killed them have been dispersed, raked out as if the roaches had come into a desert and set out in search of water, creating patterns that are terminally wavery. At the end of their lines, most are on their backs, an arc of upside-down coat buttons across the kitchen floor, their legs loose threads in the air.

Belle's mackintosh is made of plates that are disarranged, more chinks than protection. Sylvie got to the roaches before her – and found dealing with them so easy she didn't bother to mention it. Legs tapering to stilettos, Belle is precarious in the doorway. A couple of vermin are still twitching. And she's stamping, grinding at shells with her heel, leaping and crunching her way across the lino, mac flying. Dank hair-ends whip glitter in her eyes. She stops.

Her collar glints with sequins. She drops to her haunches at the fridge's metallic handle and sees reflected that her lashes are displaced horns, her skin is vile purple.

Abruptly sitting, she flicks away a corpse. She thinks she understands now what sent her neighbour packing. A ladder in her tights is an out-sized dot-to-dot line leading to her crotch. Her fingers are smeared in tart red lipstick.

She pulls the fridge door open. Each empty shelf reveals another beneath it. Except, under the freezer compartment – the handle of the plastic bag hooked over the bulb making the cold light of the fridge come out steaming red – stashed at the back are Sylvie's bottled beers.

It is 2 am. Sylvie is in the city centre, in a bus shelter.

Despite the presence tonight of Pete 'Wild Woody' Harris and the inevitability if she continues being competent of having to do a nude solo, Sylvie has as yet gone no further than her original limit of topless. For now, she can just feel pleased. At Xanadu's, on stage, in front of an audience, she danced the production number and also the finale without mistakes, indeed was so accepted she was invited for a drink in a late-night bar with colleagues Rochelle, Sue and Imo afterwards.

Her straight mouth has dimples either side, inverted commas of suppressed satisfaction.

She steps away from the bus stop and hails a taxi.

In the flat, Belle takes her make-up off and reapplies it. She puts the beer in a bowl of ice in the living room, she lounges on the sofa. She changes into something more comfortable, tucks her hair behind her ears, fluffs it round her shoulders. She changes into something less comfortable. She chucks another bottle on the pile of empties.

By the time her flatmate's key is turning in the lock, Belle has been in the bath an hour. The blanket of foam has disintegrated, the flannel over her forehead has grown cold.

The door slams shut.

'HELL-O-O!'

Belle's hair snakes over her face and neck. Around her eyes' blue cores, red is flaming. As she stands, the water comes with her momentarily before storming back into the tub.

She's almost talked herself into believing that Sylvie stole her solo. Stepping into the hall, water spreading from her feet blackens the floorboards around her. At the other end of the hall, Sylvie's bomber jacket is tight at her waist and her pink jeans skim her legs, emphasising her exquisitely proportioned figure. Belle effects the thrust-bust, thrust-arse pose, one foot slightly raised. Sylvie gives her a gummy smile.

'You waited up for me!'

Belle feels bath-water drying off her in a dowdy vest shape. She dives for Sylvie's room and spreads herself like Nell Gwyn across her flatmate's bed.

'You'll catch cold,' says Sylvie following her in. 'Here,' and she's wrapped Belle in her quilted robe.

Knees clasped, Belle stares at her toes pulled into the bedspread. The candlewick design conjures for her a freshly ploughed field, acres of gently rolling hills, with the precarious arches of her feet the beginnings of a castle. And she can almost see a knight approaching in shining armour galloping past to Sylvie.

Belle sighs. 'The man next door was asking after you.'

'That's nice.'

Belle's head is turning. 'You made quite an impression.'

'How close do you think I am to getting an Equity card?'

'Didn't you like him?'

'How much more will I have to do at Xanadu's?'

'Aren't you at least flattered?'

'How many times will I have to go nude in public?' – and Sylvie's face is in bits and Belle has cupped her hands round even while she's gathering herself together to give Sylvie a clear, straight stare.

'It won't be long before you'll be in an advert with a proper acting part exactly as you wanted.'

Belle kisses and Sylvie's forehead is so hot it feels to Belle her lips must be more coolly soothing for herself, so she's stroking Sylvie's hair and the knight is disappearing in the distance and failing to defeat the dragon anyway, and right here in reality Belle is calming her flatmate, murmuring, 'Really, sweetheart, I promise.'

Sylvie nuzzles like a puppy until she is tucked under Belle's arm, shoulder in her lap, head pillowed against Belle's breast, and Belle is frozen and sees it's the caressing while Sylvie's wide awake that's the *really* daring thing she's done, Sylvie's mouth now right by Belle's nipple, which is barely covered by the robe.

Unblinking, chin ruched, Belle stares at the blonde she's landed up in a bedroom with, whose eyelids look to her so coyly lowered. And yet, for all that time just the thought, let alone the image of a cleavage in print or celluloid, could send her red-faced, legs together writhing, now she thinks a real one's here for her caress, *demanding* her to be aroused, Belle's a block of ice. Sylvie's breasts just look like plump skin to her, soft and inviting to the touch, but just skin marked with traces of cosmetics perforated by Sylvie's open pores.

Nevertheless, it seems to Belle only polite to at least try to react enthusiastically. She tries flopping her hand round Sylvie's waist, up towards where she can feel her bra-strap cutting under her white T-shirt top. Belle clears her throat. Sylvie responds. And this is more like it, the sexy girl's fingertips are now playing with her own and – Belle feels immense relief – Belle's sensations are electric. Head twisted out of sight, she gives her lips a swift suck and stretch to make them look more fully red before . . .

Sylvie's finger has gone up to Belle's wrist. It's on the childhood scars.

'What are these from?' Sylvie wonders idly.

Framed in their separate doorways, they are divided by the hall floorboards, stretching between them.

Belle's palm remains electrified, each line distinctly hers and burning. Sylvie looks more confused than she does.

'I'm sorry,' blurts Belle and shuts her door.

At her wardrobe, she runs a finger across militaristic khaki, long vertical stripes of corporate suiting, party-pink Lycra, fur.

Pelts drape pathetically over ripped silk lining. The coat represents luxury to Belle. She puts it on, but even so, pale eyes and a crooked smile still dominate her reflection. From the top of the wardrobe she takes down a wig, lively blonde and curly. With no nylon-stocking interface, it slips.

She murmurs, 'Oooh, big boy,' and the words seem to be coming not from her but from the outfit. She purrs.

———

In his flat, Ricky Vincent is in the shower, water pounding between his shoulder blades. His face is sweaty white patched with red. His body hair is dragged into black tongues that lick diligently with the flow. His eyes are hot. His fingers work delicately. Lathering carefully with unscented soap, he partially erects his penis, rolls the foreskin back and softly splashes the pink cleaved head. Then he pulls the foreskin until there is enough slack to twist it, containing.

The shower ejects such quantities of water so fast that the sound of thundering combines with steam escaping wildly to make it seem that this cubicle is about to transport Ricky Vincent to an altogether cleaner place.

Outside, Belle's hips swing widely as her stilettos effect tiny movements along the red hall carpet. A wall light has a chance to develop and grow, to become a friendly orb beside her. The buttons of her mother's winter fur are quite secure. Bright red lipstick has seeped beyond her mouth. But it doesn't matter. The ties of the coat's lining are a bow at her waist. She knocks on Ricky Vincent's door.

In his bathrobe, Ricky opens his front door on a ragged fur coat and wig.

'For Christ's sake!'

Face pale, he's slammed the door behind her and her gash of mouth grows wider. He pinches the bridge of his nose. She grabs for his robe. He leaps back. She rolls her eyes impatiently and rips her coat off. 'Well?'

She scratches where the wig is itchy.

When she had practised her opening line in front of the mirror back home in her bedroom, alone, her eyes were hooded and she caught the final consonant of 'fuck' between her teeth. Now, her expression shapes itself into the one it's facing. Her jaw drops. Her eyes goggle. The word comes out with a farty lisp.

'How about a ff-fuck?'

His head is sinking to his hands. 'You have got to be joking.'

Shaking her head so vigorously that she displaces her wig, she splays her hands. She even deodorised her pubes and rouged her nipples for him.

Already walking away, he beckons her to follow. The condom packet she'd stashed in the heel of her stiletto has started up a blister. She limps, her naked body broken between spangly shoes and crooked wig.

In the utilities room, he wraps a sheet around her. With the corner of the sheet, he dabs her eyes and grasps her nose. 'Blow,' he instructs and she obeys.

'Better?'

She nods and takes off her wig. Hair flattened, her head looks small, except for her nose and eyes which continue to grow redder. He passes her a shirt and pair of trousers he won't mind losing.

'Put these on.'

She musters a smile. He shrugs. From the rows and rows of pine shelving of his very private walk-in cupboard, the light glows orange, a magnificent sunset of generosity. He slaps her arse. 'And now get out of here.'

At least, she thinks, it's night. Not all the street-lamps work, and in many back alleys they are few and far between. In these black ravines, only rats, rubbish bins and Belle are out.

With the stiletto heels ripped off, her shoes are boats rocking her through stormy waters. It is all the same:

Tarmac, pavement – smoothed, soothing – speed bumps, holes in the road. Cobbles. Belle stumbles.

In a modern city, cobblestones mark an area out as authentic – more *real*, more *desirable*, fundamental. It is no surprise for her to look up and see a picture of her mother on a news-stand.

There to advertise her show, Lilian White is beautiful. She is sleek and elegant.

In slacks that are too big and a shirt that has a button missing, her daughter is drowning on the street below.

chapter 7
———

*A*s autumn settles in and the sun takes a lower path across the sky, for a few afternoons for a few moments, light passes down streets and into Xanadu's foyer. The velveteen wall panels spark. In posters, girls' arms seem raised in fear. Their mauve bodies look bruised.

When it is possible to see as clearly as this, fewer punters enter. Three front-of-house staff, male and suited, are free to indulge in a small celebration.

The eldest cashier has turned 21. A couple of balloons are Sellotaped to the front desk. Behind its single black castellation, the three men are close, each smile growing by turn.

The General Manager takes his responsibilities for staff well-being very seriously. He had his wife bake a cake. He brought it in on a willow-patterned plate, which he now holds up. The General Manager's grin is so big that his cheeks touch his glasses.

'Well, son,' he says, 'blow out the candles.'

The crown of candlelight around the cake's fondant surface rises, golden, glorifying their faces.

'Yeah,' urges the younger cashier. 'Make a wish!'

The birthday boy undoes his dicky bow. He stammers, 'Th-thank you.' Then he declares, 'You're not just like family, you lot. You're better.'

Belle dashes through the foyer and up the stairs.

In the dressing room, Rochelle is showing Sue the christening present she's got for her most recent niece. Sue lays the charm bracelet across her forearm and murmurs, 'A new life is *such* a precious thing.'

Seated beside her, Mae chuckles as she tucks her hair into a nylon stocking. 'Drama queen.'

'*Moi?*' Sue wonders with mock indignation.

Laughter and teasing comments bounce easily about, until Belle enters. She nearly ballsed up the production number for everyone yesterday, and that was just her technical crime. At their mirror sections, the other girls face reflections that are intent on make-up application.

Wearing the first thing that came to hand – her mourning dress – head bowed, hands clasped before her, Belle takes small, quick steps to the middle of the room. Nearby on the fridge the kettle's boiling. Steam envelops her. She speaks up.

'Tea, anyone?'

The kettle switches itself off.

The room usually has movement everywhere, in everything – the feathers of the boas on the clothes rail, the curls of the wigs on the shelf, the swirls on the carpet, flurries of naked limbs. Now even the steam round Belle is still.

'Sue?'

Belle said 'fucking' when Sue was about to do her bridal star turn. Deep in her mirror, she draws glitter across terse lips.

'Imo?' Belle offers. 'PG, black, teaspoon of honey?'

Debs' departure left Belle's flatmate as Imo's next best ally. Tissue wielded, squeezing a blackhead, she demands, 'Where's Sylvie?'

Belle's dress matches the funereal pallor of her skin.

But then, she thinks, Mae must still be her friend – they started on the same day; they even made up after Belle nearly blew the gaff about Mae's sexuality. She steps closer.

Shifting her stool in tighter between Sue and Imo, Mae daubs violet on her eyelids.

Dress unzipped at the back, sleeves hanging round her stool's shaft, bare-breasted, Belle pulls on the head-stocking and immediately can't hear. With the auburn wig on too, she is beneath a bouffant crash helmet. But still, her hands are shaking as, blushing cheeks and all, she grease-paints out her face.

In the mirror now she sees a thick white disc, suspended. Blinking makes no impression. A mouth opened wide enough to wail is just a little hole.

She's got by all this time without friends. It was, she concludes, a silly fancy that she could like some now.

And furthermore, what she'd thought might be her backwards egg and spoon race has turned out to be a 200-metre sprint in which, for once, she is a real contender.

On the counter, her false eyelashes are splayed dead insects. Squirts of glue enliven them. The two lengths of bristle fidget on the ends of her fingers and then curve onto her lids with as sure a grip as Ricky Vincent took of her at the first rehearsal.

Ricky Vincent – who hasn't sacked and hasn't sacked her, regardless of what she's done.

The lashes' adhesive introduces a stinging to her eyes, yet no tears come. The sheer length of the lashes casts shadow awnings.

She cups her hands and hardens up the nipples, nearly ready to dance the Zone Fantastica group opener.

'Five minutes, everyone.'

But it's not the SM speaking. He hovers in the corridor behind. It is Ricky Vincent standing in the doorway, plainly dressed. His curly hair has been combed down into neat waves.

'Chop, chop,' he murmurs as another top hat and coat-tails slips past.

The white froth of Sue's bridal gown disappears around the door jamb and Belle is reflected multiply in the mirrors running round the walls as she stands and trips on the hem of her mourning dress and grabs the ledge.

She gabbles, ''M not quite ready yet, Mr Vincent, but it'll only take me a minute to get the rest of the costume on.'

The purple ceiling oppresses. Her disc of make-up turns to Ricky Vincent's face.

'Sit down, Belle.'

He sits too, their toes turned in, shoulders hunched, their

hands drooping between their laps – only, he has on a crisp white shirt. It is not just Belle's breasts that are exposed but her very life-blood as it runs through veins that lace blue across her skin. He holds her mourning dress to her so that she is more covered.

She rips it down again. She believes she sees regret.

He checks his watch. 'Perhaps I'm curious.' He has another five minutes before the others are finished on stage. 'You could have stayed at home and kept your dignity.'

'I have it here.' She sits up straight, nipples high.

'Am I going to have to spell it out for you? Y-O-U,' and she's shaking her head, 'A-R-E,' and he's carrying on, 'F-I-R-E-D.'

Belle's lashes beat down and down, the wings of a vulture coming in to rest. 'You haven't got enough girls.'

'The ones I have are pros.'

'You gave me your trousers.'

'It was you or the bin.'

'What about all that rehearsal time and effort you put in to me?' She holds her hands out to him as if they bear a pile of broken pieces.

He brushes them away. 'This is what you wanted, isn't it? Why bother acting sad?'

Damned face paint – Belle's not sad. She's angry and, more, frustrated. 'You can't, not yet!' She flaps about. 'I've got rights. I signed a contract.'

'Forget the small print, did you read the big print?'

'But why *now*? It can't be more of a risk than it was yesterday to let me out' – fuck, shit, damn, she thinks, she missed her chance – 'I could have ballsed up *totally* and there'd have been nothing you could have done to stop me, I was out there, *live*.'

He laughs. No girl can balls up so badly it can't be sorted with a quick curtain drop and a dynamic next set.

He throws a coin, portcullis flipping over queen's head enmeshing her then cutting through completely. He lets it fall to the floor and doesn't even look. He shrugs. 'Heads I win, tails too.'

But he's starting to tap his foot in irritation. Sacking someone's fun for about two seconds. He has *real* concerns tonight. It's Wild Woody's one-off special. It's meant to be a dead cert: mixed-sex shows get better takings. The Wild Woody posters made no difference to advance bookings. Ricky wants to go down and check this evening's advance sales. He's zipping Belle back into her mourning dress.

'Go feel sorry for yourself somewhere else.'

And he's pushing her towards the door.

'SM! GET THE GM AND CHUCK THIS BELLE GEORGE OUT, *NOW*!'

She stares at her raised hand which, although bare of costume, can still be a fist. And suddenly she's seeing that she could have been the punch instead of dodging round to take the one she'd made somebody else throw at her.

Frown fixed, a technician is stationed at the corridor leading to the stage. Ricky Vincent pushes her in the opposite direction. And the SM's coming down another corridor calling, '*Miss George, out the back way, fast, don't mess me.*'

Mae's in a recess. Belle's fully dressed, an outsider.

'Tina.' As if Mae's real name is a password, Belle calls louder, 'Tina Ludlow!'

Mae's neck flushes under her white disc face, her arms go up to cover her breasts. 'Can't you just fuck off and let us get on with our jobs?'

Now, before she's finished, thinks Belle – and, seeing a crack in a door, she leaps.

Pete 'Wild Woody' Harris does look remarkably like her Action Man doll, his chest shaved and sun-bed-tanned to a perfect bronzy tint, his legs apparently split parallel in manufactured joints either side of a member-less crotch. The reason it looks so strangely flat is because the fabric is stretched squarely over it by one hand down inside his G-string.

Belle sees imposed on him the back of Ricky Vincent walking away from her.

Strained up, Wild Woody's face is pink under his makeup, his free hand ready with an elastic band. And tremulously she's turned her back and half-closed her eyes and she feels through her brogues through the floor joists the live electro eight count. The thick weave of the mourning dress stimulates her nipples. And just as Ricky found the clumsy metal zipper tantalising, drawing it down, she does too. And she's in a one-foot turn that brings her facing, eyes tight shut, hands drawing the hem of her black heavy outfit up her bare thighs and teasing down and up some more and surely now – her stomach curdles – the putrid worst of her must be seething out.

She opens one eye. Wild Woody hasn't run a mile yet. Indeed, he's had to put his cloak on. And her audience has expanded too. She now has the SM staring from the doorway.

Her hip gyrations approach sensational. She slips her dress off first one shoulder, then the other, caressing back and forth before shimmying it down to reveal a perspiration-specked mound of cleavage, which she now manipulates.

Chin down, big doe-eyes sliced off by her eyebrows, she sees that the GM's here as well. He is whispering in the SM's ear.

With loud stamping, she is speeding up the eight count. The dress is off, her breasts revealed completely. In her head she can see Ricky, distant, turning. Knickers down, she makes as if to finger-fuck herself.

Wild Woody does a desperate wind-up motion with his hand. His cloak is tented a long way out. Close to laughing, she drops to a finale 'V', craning her head, which is filled with Ricky Vincent's face now huge but obscured by dark glasses. And she's upright, dodging on the spot to see round the frames, tangling herself pulling on her dress.

She urges, 'Well?'

'Impressive,' the GM mumbles. 'No music but you kept good time.'

'No, no – would you have *paid*?'

The SM shrugs. 'Don't have to.'

'But if you didn't work here, would you?'

'Sure,' assures the SM.

'Why not?' says Wild Woody.

Hands flailing as if in her effort to be cutting through the crap, she demands, '*Did you all get hard-ons?*'

The SM's eyes dodge to the GM, who tries soothing. 'Semi.'

'It's like working in a sweet shop,' explains Wild Woody carefully. 'The novelty wears off.'

Belle is falling back against a mirror section. 'I wasn't even worth applause.'

They burst into a round. But instead of it soaring her into clear blue air flying beautifully, the sound of clapping squashes her so she's not even bittily distinguishable but reduced to nothing.

She stares at Wild Woody's feet, which she sees are as precariously arched as hers. And in her head, the dark glasses have gone and the stranger's face is not awesome but merely irritated at having been interrupted doing nothing of particular importance.

The GM murmurs, 'What do you reckon?'

The SM answers, 'Yes, now. Quick.'

And as Belle is being bundled out, wrapped in the GM's raincoat, the SM checks. 'Is ten minutes enough?'

He's had to deal with worse. Wild Woody nods resignedly

'You'll get the wood *right*?' insists the SM.

'I'm a professional, aren't I?' – one hand already down his G-string.

He's to play a stud. He sighs. He's easing an elastic band down a partial erection so it won't deflate when he's on stage.

Having shut the door, the SM guards it.

Belle is on the back stairs, bag in her hands. The General Manager is above her in the doorway. He still has cake crumbs on his DJ. He flattens the hair either side of his strict parting.

'You can't stand here all night,' he says.

Her brogues, polished dark, are heavy as blocks of wood. The sleeves of her mourning dress are too short, her wrists too long, her ankles bony, her knees too knobbly. The General Manager readjusts his spectacles.

'Bye then, love,' he says.

The scraping is as portentous as if this is heaven's gate and the door closes neatly. With no handle and its security panel in an apparently unconnected recess, the entrance vanishes within the wall as if it never existed in the first place.

Outside, it is cold.

The fairy-lighted entrance of Xanadu's is flanked by the SM and a technician, who – grim-faced, arms crossed – block the entrance while girls in the Zone Fantastica poster are obscured by a board advertising tonight's one-off special, the sticker naming him 'Wild Woody' slapped on his groin.

Yet his pectorals are smooth and rounded, like breasts to look at. Hands squared, Belle's focusing on his cream-smooth jaw, his mascara-ed eyes. But she can't make him look absurd to her as he did at that rehearsal when he first turned up.

He's just seen her naked.

That's no big deal, he could have if she'd got as far performing live anyway. Right now he's miming fucking someone else on stage. She was backstage, a box of corn plasters on the Formica ledge in front of her. A piece of knicker elastic was fraying down her thigh.

She lets her eyes rise up the walls of Xanadu's – thick, windowless walls that enclose a world where anything she did or thought or wanted can seem totally remote from this outside world to her ever after. Except her face feels as blank to her as the stranger's, drawn too. And the walls of Xanadu's just keep on rising, sheering up into a dark, wet sky.

Belle first went there when it was still summer, just – when the city smelt as if the streets had been buffed with off-milk. Now it is raining. Dust is being battered down.

Gutters are blocked. Puddles are becoming pools and linking roads to pavements. Traffic has been brought practically to a standstill since flailing windscreen wipers can only rearrange the downpour. Most pedestrians are waiting, surprised, in doorways or bus shelters for it to pass.

Out in the middle of it, Belle is drenched at her thighs and across her shoulders. The raindrops are so large that instead of slaking down her skin, as they break against her, they seem momentarily to be rising, washing her away not just inside her dress but out into the world.

She passes a bar, a pub, another – and she doesn't even have to resist an urge to go in.

She's just remembered, her angel wasn't at Xanadu's tonight. Sylvie didn't see. She doesn't know.

Belle's leaping down two, four steps at a time, careering round a corner into the Underground station.

In number 12 Clover Court, in the kitchen on the red-checked table, supper is laid ready, cheese and biscuits on one side plate under Cellophane, two slices of buttered fruit cake on another by a Post-it note that says, 'Milk is in the fridge. S. xx'

At the end of the hall, Sylvie's bedroom door is open and the light looks strained through torn fabric, patching across the dark boards.

The room is almost back to how it was, all floral patterns gone, all layers of comfort such as rugs stacked to one side. Hovering, watching from the doorway, Belle feels as if a sun that was split by blackness had been coming back together, warming, thawing her just in time for her to see that it's about to set.

At the bed, bent over her suitcase, Sylvie is finishing off her packing. Her back is a Glo-white polo-neck. Her hair is in toggled bunches. When she turns, Belle sees that her eyes are far behind thick-rimmed baby blue spectacles.

Belle's murmur is desolate, 'What have I done?'

'Don't flatter yourself.'

But Belle's busy muttering, 'I know, I shouldn't have made a pass at you . . .'

Sylvie's laughing. '*That's* what it was.'

'The state of the flat, then, if I'd cleaned before you moved in, warned you about the cockroaches . . .' The possibility of action brings her suddenly in to Sylvie's room. 'I *will* clear up – new bed, new curtains, just tell me what you want, I'll get it.' Arm braced, she's stopping her flatmate closing her suitcase. 'New fridge? Electric kettle?'

Sylvie's fighting for control of her luggage. 'It's nothing to do with you. I'd applied to college back home. Drama course. I called my mum. I've got a place.'

'You're leaving Xanadu's too?'

'I'm leaving London.'

'It *wasn't* me.'

'Nothing to do with you at all.' But Belle's grip is still tight on her suitcase buckle. Sylvie's voice is coaxing. 'I mean, yeah, sure, I'd never in a million years have let my worst enemy live in the state this flat was in, but, well, horses for courses. Just because I don't like your standards of hygiene doesn't mean I don't like you.' She slams the case shut.

'You're not offended. You're not disgusted.'

'Blimey,' says Sylvie, dragging her suitcase off the bed. 'I mean, I will be if you want but truly, no.'

Belle almost looks defeated, 'Will you be in touch?'

'Maybe.' Sylvie looks down. She looks straight back. 'More likely not. Listen. You gave me a cheap place to stay, so thanks. A lot, for real. And we had fun. And now I'm going.' Sylvie lifts a hand. She mocks a wave. '"Bye." See? It's easy. You try.'

Belle's laughter floods her throat as tears. 'I'd have rather got back and found you'd gone.'

'I'm touched. I had no idea I meant so much. But my ticket's only valid for this train and it leaves in three quarters of an hour.'

Sylvie flings her arms round Belle and is kissing her on the lips and Belle is stumbling ahead for more, deeper into an empty room, her body seeming to be hurtling itself through a hoop, and she feels she's hardly had a chance to stand before she's trying to land herself through another hole, again, another.

'I'll miss you!' – and Belle doesn't think it would be possible for her to humiliate herself much further and after all the world hasn't collapsed around her.

Sylvie's standing impatient in the doorway. Belle arcs her mouth and brows in different directions. 'Oh well.'

Together, they pull Sylvie's suitcase down the hall.

At the door, Sylvie asks, 'Will you be all right?'

Belle looks surprised to be answering, 'Yes. And you?'

Sylvie's nod is vigorous. 'My worry was my fees, and my mum's got me a fill-in job at the salon.'

––––––

Tonight is the last of Lilian White's new television series.

Backstage, overhead along the ceiling, the fluorescent strip is narrowed by perspective, pointing. At the end is Lilian, her hair rolled and pinned into a crown of reflecting light. Her dress, minuscule about her body, trails regally. She glides while crew, staff and fans leap and stumble to keep up.

At a split in the corridor, in her black mourning dress, Belle merges easily with the shadows. Her presence is little more than a scent of damp from the outside world.

During broadcasts, Lilian remains unapproachable, safe from the viewers within television sets in living rooms around the country. It is easy for her to keep cool through her performances. Now, on the ground, sweat breaks out at her temples even while her shoulder straps stretch her shoulders wider, stronger apart, and seaming scoops her waist strictly in.

At one time, pregnancy swelled her belly and breasts, unpredictably.

Belle calls quietly, 'Mummy.'

Maintaining a full professional smile, Lilian commands over her shoulder, 'OLIVER, EVERYONE: I'LL BE WITH YOU IN QUARTER OF AN HOUR.'

And suddenly – 'Aren't you ashamed?' – Belle's hearing Geoffrey's words in her head – '*ashamed*?' – and she's shaking her head, rat-tails flailing, and she's staring wide-eyed at her brogues which are caked grey, her dress hem too, her fingernails, and she knows like this of course she'll make her mother wince. And now she's trying to scrape the mud off her shoes with one heel then the other, but she's seeing Ricky Vincent – semen sticky on her mourning dress – Mae's painted laugh, her tough workmate's bare breasts in the crooks of her elbow. She looks up.

Belle is presented with a face so beautiful and fragile it could be porcelain in mid-air.

'Lilian.'

And Lilian does wince. Normally Belle might be relieved to get a definite reaction.

'Did you see the show?'

'Tonight especially I wish I had, but I couldn't, I'm sorry – I was at Xanadu's.'

Lilian tries – briefly listen, make a link to somewhere else – but porcelain's cracking '*For Christ's sake! Do you want me to forbid you?*'

And now the cracks are gaping and Lilian is back in the

unwed mother's home, her feet in stirrups, men in white masks removing something from inside her and taking it away.

It was understood. A child born out of wedlock had to be adopted. But with a post-birth rush of adrenalin, Lilian unexpectedly knew.

'*I want to keep my baby.*'

They brought it back and it was hideous, purple and screaming. And its anger didn't abate.

Her hands are at her face shaking as if to repair the damage.

'At *your* age, I'd become a single mother and re-established my career.'

And I, thinks Belle, have just finger-fucked myself in front of total strangers.

'At *your* age . . .'

Lilian defied convention, felt she'd acted virtuously, even heroically, got fearful nights, no medal.

What about the father?

He was merely careless.

She risked her family's good name, had to create her own.

'Why are you doing this to me, *why*?'

And Belle is seeing herself in the dressing room, with the GM and the SM and Wild Woody all embarrassed for her but mainly desperate to get her out.

Belle was a cause of shame before she was a source of joy.

In trying to side-step the hole, Lilian kept them both constantly aware that it was there.

And the last thing Belle wants is to give Lilian still more reason to panic about how things just keep on falling in and no amount of castle walls, applause can stop it happening.

Lilian is shaking Belle. 'I KEPT YOU.'

Belle is shaking Lilian harder. 'EVERYTHING'S ALL RIGHT, I GOT SACKED.'

And Lilian falls free, her breathing heavy.

She laughs weakly. 'A daughter of mine should at least have had the presence of mind to resign.'

Lilian stares down at Belle's sleeve. And even as she touches its tattiness she looks afraid that she'll be lost.

Perhaps after all it's not Lilian who stole the limelight but the limelight that stole her. Belle slides her fingers down her mother's dress and finds in the smooth, fine silk a snag and would usually on instinct be practically on her knees to tie it up, so she can stand and lean her full weight against the figure of her mother. She leaves the snag.

Lilian is waiting.

Belle takes her hand. It doesn't slip away but grasps back tightly.

Gaps unfilled, distinctly part of each of them and staying that way, mother and daughter are fluted columns, simply standing for a moment, side by side.

———

At Xanadu's, Wild Woody is waiting in the wings.

Inside his G-string, because of the way the elastic band cuts in, an ill-fitting ring, too tight, ruching his skin at the base, his penis looks stuck on, like just another prop to take on stage – nothing to do with him. He stares into the spotlight and pumps his chest muscles, ready to play King.

A courtesan beside him, Imo murmurs, 'Good luck.'

'Thanks. You too.'

The music leads them on.

Outside, the rain has stopped. The sky is clear.

Catching the street-light, puddles splashing out round Belle's shoes are sparks showering from a blow torch she could take with her anywhere to burn through anything.

Back in her apartment, Lilian sits on the antique sofa in her silk peacock robe. She has a photograph album in her lap, open on a full-page portrait of her adult daughter.

Stashed at the back of a filing cabinet drawer, there are several contact sheets, dozens of miniatures in which Belle, posing on a stool, looks uncomfortable, ready to sneeze, sad. In this one, Belle is beautiful. Her eyes are open and trusting, her smile is carefree. Lilian strokes her fingertips across the picture. It is two dimensional. Lilian shuts the

album. Even as she chides herself for wasting energy, she
weeps.

––––––––

Apart from the exit, which rises from the asphalt surface
like a ship's funnel, the roof of Clover Court is deck-flat.
And although the block is only twelve storeys, not much
near is higher, so the view beyond the railings that run
round the edge is of little else but sky. Sitting cross-legged
in the middle on a folded coat, Belle wouldn't be surprised
to taste salt on her lips or to look out and see a seagull flying
by. Except it's night.

The breeze is a caress around her face but also bracing.
The cold of it keeps the blood working at the surface of her
skin. Eyes closed, she passes a hand across her head, into the
dip at the back of her neck, over the hard, almost square top
of her skull, and her hair feels velvety, neither aggressive
nor lavishly feminine but a length that seems to her somewhere in between.

She used sharp scissors this time, blades flashing light
around the bathroom where she'd set up mirrors that let her
see clearly from every angle what she was doing. The fringe
just needed tidying up. She used her fingers like an ivory
comb through the long split-ends to spread them flat in sections that she could slice off cleanly. Curled, they formed a
nest in her hand, warming till she could almost feel the lines
of her palm growing deeper, more secure. And the cut hair
lapped over her wrists' scars of childhood slips from bikes, of
knives, covering them, seeming to Belle to be erasing softly.

The blanket her mother made is luxurious around Belle's arms and shoulders. Through the crocheted holes when Belle holds them up she can see stars twinkling. And the strands of wool seem to be disintegrating in her fingers. The blanket falls away from her as she steps towards the railings to see the streets below lit as if for a party. Neon shop signs flash, car headlamps beam out as disco strobes.

Sounds are brought by winds that are lengths of silk caressing her alternately. She can choose which piece to wrap herself in. A dog howls gloomily. An ambulance arcs by, sirens wailing. A couple of female teenage voices start up singing.

Belle leans over, hands clutched, quiet as the girls lurch happily from pop – 'I wanna be the one' – to gospel – 'Oh Lord you are the one' – enjoying ambitious, off vibratos and breaking for laughter, before settling into practising choir parts. With just two voices, the girls can manage only a gappy serenade. Their bursts of sound and text seem meaningless in isolation. But from the singing girls, rising through the air, Belle hears a soft hand-clapping too.

Now you can order superb titles directly from Virago

☐	Poker Face	Josie Barnard	£7.99
☐	The Things We Do to Make it Home	Beverly Gologorsky	£6.99
☐	The Cure for Death by Lightning	Gail Anderson-Dargatz	£6.99
☐	A Rough Guide to the Heart	Pam Houston	£7.99
☐	Man Crazy	Joyce Carol Oates	£7.99
☐	The Pleasing Hour	Lily King	£6.99

The prices shown above are correct at time of going to press. However, the publishers reserve the right to increase prices on covers from those previously advertised, without further notice.

Virago

Please allow for postage and packing: **Free UK delivery.**
Europe: add 25% of retail price; Rest of World: 45% of retail price.

To order any of the above or any other Virago titles, please call our credit card orderline or fill in this coupon and send/fax it to:

Virago, PO Box 121, Kettering, Northants NN14 4ZQ
Fax: 01832 733076   Tel: 01832 737526
Email: aspenhouse@FSBDial.co.uk

☐ I enclose a UK bank cheque made payable to Virago for £ . . . .
☐ Please charge £ . . . . . . to my Visa/Access/Mastercard/Eurocard

Expiry Date ☐☐☐☐   Switch Issue No. ☐☐

NAME (BLOCK LETTERS please) . . . .

ADDRESS . . . .

. . . .

. . . .

Postcode . . . . Telephone . . . .

Signature . . . .

Please allow 28 days for delivery within the UK. Offer subject to price and availability.

Please do not send any further mailings from companies carefully selected by Virago ☐